Where the Yellow Violets Grow

A WWII Historical Romance

based on the letters of Lieutenant Janet Castner
Special credits to Mary Morrissey Gardner

Edited by Samantha Bohrman and Cristina Pippa

Map by John Renehan

Cover design by Les Solot Les

D.L. Gardner

D.L. Gardner

Port Orchard, WA

Where the Yellow Violets Grow
D.L. Gardner
ISBN 9781386236221

Copyright © 2018 by D.L. Gardner

All rights reserved. No part of this publication may be reproduced, distributed or transmitted in any form or by any means, including photocopying, recording, or other electronic or mechanical methods, without the prior written permission of the publisher, except in the case of brief quotations embodied in critical reviews and certain other noncommercial uses permitted by copyright law. For permission requests, write to the publisher, addressed "Attention: Permissions Coordinator," at the address below.

D.L. Gardner
Port Orchard WA
http://gardnersart.com

Publisher's Note: This is a work of fiction. Some names and characters, places, and incidents are actual, some are created from the author's imagination. Locales and public names are sometimes used for atmospheric purposes. Any resemblance to actual people other than those the author has permission to use, living or dead, or to businesses, companies, events, institutions, or locales is completely coincidental.

Book Layout ©2017 BookDesignTemplates.com

Contact Ingram Sparks for ordering information.

Where the Yellow Violets Grow/ D.L. Gardner. -- 1st ed.

This book is dedicated to Mary Morrissey Gardner whose encouraging words, and loving heart is the major reason this book was created.

Maybe we'll be home by Christmas. It's so lovely in Pennsylvania at Christmas time. And then you and I could walk in the woods. The forest is beautiful in the winter. I'll show you where the yellow violets grow. We'll dig in the snow and find the trailing arbutus. They have a lovely fragrance.

-Lieutenant Janet Castner

Contents

Lieutenant Janet Castner 8

Technical Sergeant Lou Morrissey 23

Darkest Before Dawn 28

Morning Reminder 38

Major Billet 53

Father Dean 64

Lieutenant Frost 67

A Moonlit Meeting 73

Cookies 79

Tell me 84

Dobi 96

Gift of a Moment 115

The Pit of War 122

The Officer's Dance 127

Solace 135

All about CBI 143

The Antique Shoppe 153

Hard Benches 160

Light Against the Dark 171

Where is She? 177

Scotland 182

Grace in the Line of Fire 190

Persuasion 201

Jack	223
Interruption	229
On Trial	233
Billet	**Error! Bookmark not defined.**
The Enemy	242
Lou's Turn	248
Deshon	261
Zoey	265
Apology	276
Holiday	281
A Partridge in a Pear Tree	288
January 1945	293
March 1945	301
April 1945	307
Surrender	312
Epilogue	317

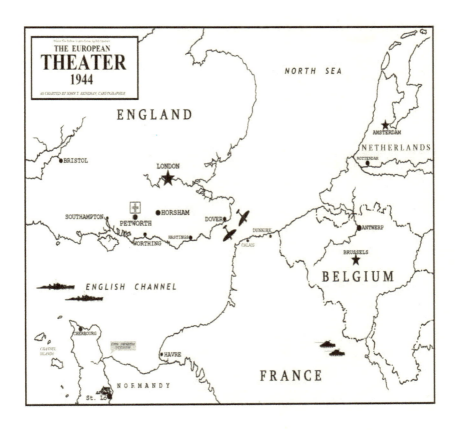

D.L. Gardner

Chapter 1

Lieutenant Janet Castner

January 1944

> *Your country is at war and faces just such a situation as the First Reserve of the American Red Cross Nursing Service is intended to meet ... Millions of our men are in service in this country and overseas. It is your privilege and patriotic duty to give them the care they so justly deserve by accepting an assignment with the Army Nurse Corps. —Mary Beard, Director of Nursing Services, 1944*

Petworth wasn't the quaint little British town Lieutenant Janet Castner had seen in tourist brochures before she left the States. No. The images she had thumbed through at the L.A. County Library during the months she was training, before she embarked on that great voyage to Europe, gave a completely different impression. According to those images, flower baskets would hang from white framed windows overlooking narrow cobblestone alleys, and ivy would drape over red brick walls. Young girls in pinafores would play hopscotch on sidewalks or jump rope on freshly mowed lawns. Boys in knee-britches with their newsboy caps and bow ties would shoot marbles in front of barber shops or play tag in the street.

To her disappointment, she saw none of that from the backseat of the motor coach

The cab came to a halt.

"This is it?" Janet asked.

"Looks like," her friend Martina Alvarez responded. A tall Hispanic nurse anesthetist with whom Janet had become good friends, rolled down her window.

"The road's in ruins, miss. The coach won't roll through this wreckage," the cab driver proclaimed in a thick British accent. He pushed back his cap, looked over his shoulder, and gave them a hearty grin.

"I'm sure this is the way to the hospital," Janet argued as she pulled her map from her bag.

"Yes, ma'am. But you can't get there by car."

Janet sighed heavily. "So, we have to walk with all our luggage? There are twenty-five nurses behind us."

"There's a footpath through this rubble that will take you and your twenty-five nurses to where you need to go," he offered, though he didn't show the way.

"Great," Lieutenant Evelyn Dobi mumbled under her breath. Younger than any of the nurses that had flown from

Scotland to Petworth on this assignment, she was a stocky woman with a cynical outlook on life. Her pessimism bothered even Janet, a master of buoyancy. Dobi leaned against the seat, a pout on her face, and crossed her hands over her chest.

"Hey, we get a chance to put into practice what we've trained for, you know?" Marty offered with a grin and slid out of the car. "I, for one, can't wait to get out of this vehicle and get some fresh air!"

Janet followed Marty's lead and pulled her suitcase from the taxi's trunk. Soon the band of nurses, baggage in hand, stood together in the wet and rainy landscape. Once the caravan of taxis drove away, Janet stepped away from the others, expecting to hear people, chickens or dogs, or some other sound that would indicate that the city of Petworth had living inhabitants.

She heard nothing. Nor did she breathe in a pleasing odor of fresh ocean breeze, lilacs or rose that she had expected of a parish so near the English Channel. Rain and mud and wet cement were the only pungent fragrances.

"This is not what I expected," Janet whispered to Marty.

"I didn't know what to expect, however there is a war going on, Janet," Marty assured her. "Of that we were forewarned!"

"You're right. I'm just belly aching over my first taste of discomfort. I'm sure there will be a lot more to follow." She surveyed the demolished landscape. "Of which I won't have the privilege to complain about."

Hovering clouds grayed the earth, the wind threatened to steal Janet's cap, and a rubble of broken buildings loomed over her. Janet fastened the top button to her coat and saluted the lone officer who appeared out of the mist.

"Lieutenants! I see you've made it here early!" The man returned the salute. His dark coat rustled in the breeze. The wool scarf he wore around his neck protected his ears, though his face flushed from cold. A pleasant sight, his eyes beamed blue, a stark contrast against the gray of the weather and the disturbing ruins surrounding them.

"Sir!" Janet stepped forward. "I'm Lieutenant Castner." She introduced herself and glanced at the other nurses.

"Lieutenant James Frost here." Lieutenant Frost's smile spilled out like a sun peeking behind the clouds. "Welcome to Petworth. I'm afraid this road to the hospital hasn't yet been repaired, but we're working on it. We should have it cleaned up by the time the other nurses arrive. There is another road to the hospital in better shape than this, but it's much longer and hard on tires. I doubt your driver found it worth the risk." He nodded at the scattered wreckage as he picked up Janet and Marty's suitcases. "We'll have to walk from here. Follow me."

Janet slipped over the uneven footpath that had been carved through broken brick and crushed stone. She swapped her gaze from the gray ash and powder that clung to her shoes, to the debris surrounding her. Burnt beams lay scattered against half-standing walls. Broken furniture hid amongst the rubble. A leg from a table extended into space, the rest of its body buried under blocks of cement, granite, and gravel. Electrical wires rocked dangerously in the rain. Roofless structures grasped for the cloudy sky, their window frames sticking out against the fog, the glass demolished and long gone.

"What kind of building was this?" Marty asked.

"A boys' school," Frost answered. "Further ahead you'll see the remains of the chapel."

"Good heavens! When was it bombed?" Janet wiped the mist that had accumulated on her brow. She knew of the bombing blitz in London, and how the Germans nearly destroyed the city. She hadn't been aware that the people of Sussex had been victim to the assault as well.

"Two years ago. September 29, 1942."

"Are they still bombing this area?" Marty asked.

"Who knows?" Lieutenant Frost chuckled quietly to himself. "The Germans bomb whatever they damn well please."

Janet and Marty exchanged a worried glance.

"Expect blackouts. There's a shelter at the base–a dugout of sorts."

A hundred yards away, amid freshly cut grass and tombstones, a towering stone cross hovered over a graveyard. Fresh cut flowers decorated the memorial, propped up by vases. A toy soldier had been placed at one of the headstones. "A child?"

"Twenty-eight children to be exact, the headmaster and a teacher. Once you meet the residents of Petworth, I'm sure you'll hear the stories. Even though it happened two years ago, the town still grieves. No one ever forgets their children."

"I wasn't aware of Petworth being a target," Janet whispered as she read the other headstones.

"The chapel was also destroyed. If any of your nurses are looking for a place to worship, you'll have to visit Father Dean at the old 48th General Hospital, adjacent to ours. He's set up a makeshift sanctuary in one of the huts. You'll enjoy Father Dean. Nice guy."

They hiked away from the ruins through an open field of clover and dried thistle. Long strands of wild grass leaned from the weight of the rain, carpeting the valley with a golden hue. In the center of these plains nested a settlement of rusty cylindrical buildings covered with corrugated steel.

"Quonset huts?" Sue had been traveling with Janet ever since she enlisted in Pennsylvania. "We had those in California. I was afraid we'd be staying in tents!"

"Not quite tents." The lieutenant laughed. "These are Nissen huts. Smaller than the American Quonsets, but with a different interior structure. I think you'll find them more suited to British weather," Frost explained.

"Drier then?" Sue asked.

"Does the sun ever shine in Britain?" Marty pulled the tip of her hat further over her face and covered her cheeks with her coat collar.

Janet scanned the sky, hoping to see a break in the clouds. Instead, five Mosquito bombers appeared like bees, their sound breaking the silence like a sheet of glass busting in an echo chamber. They buzzed low overhead toward the channel. Toward France. A reminder that very soon she and her nurses would be meeting the Face of War.

Everyone stopped and watched, and Janet couldn't help but eye Dobi and the other nurses who had fallen behind. Though the Army trained her well, the sight of the bombers brought home a cold reality. She wondered how her nurses would react to an influx of wounded soldiers from a war zone, especially young Dobi.

"Look," Marty whispered and nodded toward a group of children playing tag in the fields. "At least some hearts are light enough to laugh."

The children were not far away, closer to the hospital than the village. Three boys and two girls. They came to a halt when they saw the officers. The boys stood at attention and saluted. Lieutenant Frost returned their salute with a grin. Janet caught the eye of one little girl. A sandy-haired child with pigtails and bows. How much paler the British children were than kids in America, she thought. The girl stared at Janet in wonderment. The closer Janet came, the more the child blushed until, with a gasp, she bent her knee and curtsied.

"Odd," Sue whispered.

Lieutenant Frost glanced at Janet, and then the child, but he said nothing.

Soon they descended the hill to an orderly row of corrugated steel huts.

The buildings could not have been more military in appearance—drab green, white circles with large red crosses on their doors and on their roofs. The huts were positioned in a pattern. Three rows forward and three cross-wise. Perhaps fifty of such huts in all, and five skeletons of the same in various stages of construction.

"Here you are, ladies. Your station and your quarters. This hut holds the medical supplies and three nurses." He set the suitcases down and opened the door for them. "The next three huts accommodate up to twenty-five nurses each. Once you're settled, I'll give you an orientation. Some of the huts have just been built and we're moving beds and medical equipment into them this afternoon. You'll need to know where the wards are. Lieutenant Castner?"

"Yes, sir."

"I understand your experience is with orthopedics. Major Billet informs me you'll be supervisor in that ward."

"He did?" Startled, Janet had no idea she'd be put in such an important position so quickly.

"Is there a problem?" Lieutenant Frost asked.

"No! I'm sorry, I just wasn't aware. I mean, why me?"

"From what the Major tells me, you have an excellent reputation as a leader. It's all on your resume and your referrals. Your personal barracks will be in the supply hut. There are three beds in there."

"I'm assuming Major Billet is our commanding officer?" Sue inquired.

"Yes. He's in London right now. Major McCall is acting commander. He's a hard-liner, so be on your toes."

"How many patients do we have?" Janet asked.

"None now. We're just setting up. The hospital used to be a WWI base and is in want of repair and more huts are being built. We're expecting wounded any day now, so there's a lot of work to do." He gave Janet a salute along with a wide and handsome smile. "See you soon." He led the other nurses to the adjacent hut.

"What a cutie!" Sue whispered in Janet's ear. "Did you notice those dimples?"

"He's a fine-looking man," Janet agreed. "But this place is a mess!" Janet put her hands on her hips and shook her head. Indeed, the hut, though nearly empty, was laced with cobwebs and dust. The inside had been painted the same army green as the outside, and paint peeled away near the seams where rust corroded the walls. Lightbulbs hung over each cot, though there were only three in this hut. The rest of the room included a kitchen area, a closet, and a row of ice boxes.

"I was hoping the inside of this hut would look better than the outside. I'm significantly disappointed. Look at these windows! They haven't been washed since the last war!" Marty snickered.

"If then," Sue added.

"I'm not sure they wanted clean windows. I think they were using this place for target practice," Janet suggested.

"It does appear that way, doesn't it?" Sue inched her way down the aisle to one of the beds. Her lips curled in disgust. "Iron cots with straw mattresses? Straw? And no linen anywhere to be seen. Nor pillows."

"What? No pillow?" Marty's half pout broke into a grin. "That is roughing it."

Sue tossed her suitcase on one of the beds. "At least there's a Limey stove in the middle of the room? Who's going to chop wood?"

"I'll do it," Marty offered. "You wash my clothes."

"Ha! Looks like we'll be doing that in a bucket!"

"I'm sure there are bedsheets and blankets somewhere." Janet pulled open the doors to the many iceboxes. Some were supplied with plasma and penicillin, others needed to be stocked.

"Did you see this propane cookstove?" Marty pulled open the oven door, tested for dust with her finger, and made a face at the grease left on her hand.

"No lie? An oven? We can cook our own meals!" The idea made Janet giggle. A long time had passed since she practiced her cooking skills. "You know what this means, don't you? Homemade fudge. Pies. Goodies galore!"

"You and your sweet tooth, Janet," Marty admonished her teasingly. "Just give me steak and eggs."

"Oh golly, Marty, did you have to mention meat? I'm so starved for protein I could eat a cow on the hoof."

"Sorry, ladies. The word is that Britain's on rations," Janet reminded them. "No meat. Certainly, no steaks! We might be able to find a local farmer in town with chickens, and barter him out of some eggs. Sweets it will have to be."

"If England doesn't run out of sugar," Sue mumbled.

The drone of a German bomber soaring overhead drowned out her voice. Janet shut the door to the icebox quickly and turned to the other women in the room. Faces paled, eyes wide as they listened. "How far are we from London?" Janet asked.

"Forty miles, thereabouts," Marty answered.

"Are you sure they don't bomb hospitals?" The dread in Sue's eyes matched that in Janet's heart.

Janet shook her head. "According to the Geneva convention, they aren't supposed to."

"Well, that's reassuring!"

"Look, we're in a war zone. We knew it was going to be dangerous. We signed up for this."

More aircraft silenced them. Sue raced to the door to look out.

"Is it ours?"

"I don't know. All I saw was a tail disappear into the clouds."

Janet stood next to her, listening to the rumble of the aircraft until it diminished, replaced by the gentle sound of rain dripping from the gutters. "Well," she said. "You can bet your curlers that won't be the last bomber to fly over our little hospital. We'll be seeing a lot more of the war, so come to terms with your fears now, ladies, because even if this little hospital isn't bombed, we'll be taking care of the men who are. Can you imagine what our GIs will think if they see us cringe whenever a plane flies over?"

Janet presumed both Marty and Sue's thoughts ran along the same line as hers—that they were in for an experience of a lifetime. No one spoke as they chose their beds, unpacked quietly, and then explored further their new home.

Sue pulled out a stack of linen from the wall closet and handed a set of sheets to Marty. When she brought linens to Janet, she sat on the bed next to her. "Answer me a riddle, please."

"What's that?"

"When we were walking through the field and that little English girl saw you, why in the world did she curtsy? I can understand the boy saluting, but is it common for British children to curtsy when they see American nurses?"

"No, silly." Marty laughed as she tucked her blanket in tight and straightened the wrinkle with a sweep of her hand. "That's something British people do for royalty. Haven't you seen princess Elizabeth in her uniform? She and Janet could be twins."

Janet met Sue's gaze as Marty continued.

"I mean, aside from the fact that Janet is wearing a US Red Cross uniform and Princess Elizabeth wears a reserve uniform."

Janet felt a fever rush to her face as Sue stared at her.

"Holy to Betsy, I never noticed that before! What kind of ghosts are in your closet, Janet?" Sue exclaimed.

Not a subject Janet wanted to discuss. This wasn't the first time she'd been told she looked like Princess Elizabeth. She shrugged it off as coincidence.

"Speaking of closets, were there any cleaning supplies in that one?" Janet asked. She frowned at Sue's bewilderment. "We've got to scrub this hut down, make our beds and inspect the condition of the other wards by tomorrow before our nurses get here. I have a feeling no one's used this place since the Canadians left. When was that? Two years ago?"

"I was just wondering—" Sue began, but Janet quieted her with a scowl.

That evening, orders were to keep the windows shaded, so Janet wrote a letter to her sister by candlelight.

Dear Flo,

I arrived safely in Petworth. All my expectations have been quashed. The village may be quaint, but there is wreckage from a recent bombing here where twenty-eight children were killed. I pity the poor people who lost their babies, and the memories they must have of that horrid event.

I'm sure the countryside is pretty in the spring, but right now the skies are gray and everything else has absorbed the same dullness. I can't tell if it's only the weather, or also the war that makes England so dismal. I suspect both.

I have close friends now who I trained with, and we are all here in the hospital ready to work. I also met a very kind man, Lieutenant Frost, who is giving us a grand tour.

Tomorrow we straighten up these little huts that haven't seen a mop for two years. I'll be happy to settle in and start mending our wounded soldiers. It's been awhile since I've been doing any nursing what with all this marching around like a foot soldier! I'm sure the adventure that awaits will be more than I ever imagined. I just hope I can be a good samaritan for the war effort, although as soon as I arrived I wished even more that the war were over. Please write me and let me know how things are at home. I miss you.

Keep me informed if you are still considering joining the Corps. Maybe I can give you some advice.

Your sister, Janet

P.S. Aside from the marching drills, Scotland was lovely!

 Chapter 2

Technical Sergeant Lou Morrissey

D-Day June 6, 1944

Soldiers, Sailors, Airmen of the Allied Expeditionary Force! You are about to embark upon the Great Crusade, toward which we have striven these many months. The eyes of the world are upon you... Your task will not be an easy one. Your enemy is well trained, well equipped, and battle hardened. He will fight savagely. —General Dwight D. Eisenhower.

Indeed, the eyes of the world are upon us! General Eisenhower's words rattled like a machine gun in Lou Morrissey's mind. "If only the eyes of the world had been a bit more discriminatory! Things would have worked out better if the Germans weren't so attentive," Lou whispered as he bent low and ran through the wet sand on Omaha Beach. Cannon balls exploded indiscriminately around him, machine gunfire ripped through the lines of men racing for cover. Bombs detonated. Grenades shattered a tank a few feet away.

The soldier running next to him tumbled to the ground, his jacket soaked in blood.

"Don't let your men stop," the captain came up from behind. "Run. Run like there is no tomorrow, because if you stop, there won't be."

Lou sprinted on, giving a nod to his men to follow. His breath short, his lungs hot, the sand deep. A thick screen of rifle, machine-gun and mortar fire poured at them with deadly accuracy, and at the thousands of other soldiers invading the Normandy. The ground rumbled and shook as if the earth itself were about to burst. Dust and fire mushroomed into the glowering sky. Grey clouds of ash and smoke spat down from the sky, blackening the raging sea. The troops dodged death, burrowing wherever they could. There was no place to run to. Lou dove behind a smoldering jeep, the assault too intense to continue. He dug, scraping at the sand with the butt of his rifle, and slid into the cavity. There he waited, covering his ears. Cramped like a sardine, shoulder to shoulder with two other men, he stooped as low as he could, avoiding the shells of allied destroyers off shore and enemy mortar from the crags above.

He didn't see one German, only smoke and fire flaring out from behind the fuming hillside, and long dark slits in the side of the cliff where the enemy field guns hid. No Germans, though. Only their massive weaponry front.

The division circled behind the 2nd Ranger Battalion and scaled the 100-foot bluffs that day. With potato-mashers and a bazooka, the allied forces obliterated the artillery that the U.S. Navy hadn't destroyed.

When the assault stilled, the troops were ordered to stay low.

Lou resigned himself to watching the fog roll inland and listening to the pounding breakers of a dark and agitated sea. Even though the artillery fire had stopped, and the bombings had ceased, the hammering still resounded as if thunder had been jailed in his head and split his skull with bolts of lightning. Shutting his mind to the horror of the battle, he relived the conversation that led him to France.

Three years ago, he and Jack Diersing had made the decision to enlist. Jack, his best friend for nineteen years had been by his side anytime something important had happened. His first Little League home run, Jack cheered in the batter's cage. As Boy Scouts, they pitched tents together under the stars at Camp Freidlander. Both Jack and Lou performed altar boy duties at St. Mary's Church. And they graduated high school together. Why wouldn't they serve their country together?

The two had been talking war maneuvers one night at the local pub, Tin Front in East Hyde Park. Discussing strategy over tap and offering tactical advice to any eavesdropper who cared to hear, they laid out a blueprint to solve the world's problems! Jack held his mug up to Lou, foam seething over its rim and splashing onto the bar. "We spent our young lives cracking the case for peace over a glass of milk when we were tikes, ginger ale in grade school, and now beer. By golly, I think it's about time we get to making a real difference, you and I."

Lou met his toast. They'd been together so long and were so close that Lou read his mind. "Infantry?" he asked as their glasses chimed in agreement.

"Face to face with the enemy," Jack said. "On the ground, where we can see the whites of their eyes!"

And so, it was.

Lou sighed, watching the fog thicken and hover overhead, Jack's words a whisper on his lips. No whites of the eyes. And Jack had been moved to a different division. Was it even possible for the two of them to make a difference? Could anyone?

With dawn came the rustling of men and an order to rise. He pulled himself together, grabbed his pack and his gun.

"Let's go," he said to the others—his men, his charges—now scattered across the hillside and on the beach below. The exhausted, smelly bodies, the remnant of the 29th Division, crawled past rows of trenches, clumsily kicking dirt in the already sand-filled mouths of the men below them. Lou's desire to see daylight and breathe fresh air dissipated once he stood. Shapes bulged along the shoreline as dawn crept over the horizon. A continuing mass of refuse floated on the surf beyond—scattered remnants of invasion paraphernalia. Overturned and blown apart trucks and tanks. A blackened beach. The looming smell of gunpowder. Half sunk boats.

Splintered remains of unidentifiable forms. A solemn silence enveloped the coastline as the living stepped over the dead, carefully, soberly. Gravely. Litter-bearers would come and lift the bodies on stretchers and send them home. Today the war had not been won. Today he, and those remaining men he fought with, would march on. Beyond Normandy.

Chapter 3

Darkest Before Dawn

Janet had never worked so hard in her life the day the GIs from Normandy were brought in. Hundreds of patients within a matter of hours filled the Nissen huts. Jeeps, lorries, trucks and ambulances brought the wounded, and helicopters flew in the more serious cases. Janet worked ten-hour days, and sometimes double shifts. Extra staff from London, Horsham, and Worthing arrived to help with the influx, taking some patients to other hospitals along the Channel, and to London. Two weeks passed with no relief, and finally most of the patients were either healed, or had been transferred.

Exhausted, and ready for a change of scene, Janet put in a request for a leave. Even though Marty and Sue had theirs, her consent for a leave didn't arrive until mid-September.

"Well what do you know? I finally got it!" Janet held her papers in the air. Marty slammed her book closed, and Sue jumped from her bed.

"Good going, Miss!" Sue said. "Just in time. We rented a room for this weekend."

"It took them long enough to get this to you." Marty took the papers from Janet and read. "Why did you have to wait so long?"

"You know how mail is," Sue said.

"It's just as well. You saw how busy we were. They needed us." Janet folded up her papers and pulled her suitcase from under the bed.

"It's going to be warm this weekend. We're thinking beach," Sue reminded her. "Bring your suit and bathing cap."

The three of them walked into the better part of Petworth, where structures still stood untouched by war. Thrilled that the romantic postcard village really did exist, they explored the cobblestone streets, had a delicious British dinner at a quaint little café, took in a movie— *Our Hearts Were Young and Gay*—and spent the night in a simple but elegant room with magnificent antiques overlooking the city square.

"What a fun movie." Janet topped the stairs and unlocked the bedroom door. "I enjoyed laughing for a change."

"I can relate, though," Sue said.

"What do you mean?"

"Well, think about it. Haven't we missed the boat like those gals in the motion picture?" Sue set her purse on the dresser.

"Ha! You mean like as far as men go?" Marty asked, letting her silky black hair fall over her shoulders when she took the bobby pins out. "I'd hate to think I'm going to be a spinster for the rest of my life." She unscrewed a wine bottle.

"Me too!" Sue agreed.

"Don't be silly. You have to be old and unmarried to be a spinster," Janet said.

"Well I'm not getting any younger, that's for sure. I found a gray hair this morning." Sue searched her locks to find the gray.

"That's probably just the war doing that to you. Stress!" Janet teased.

Marty giggled. "That's one way to look at it. Care for a glass of wine?" She kicked off her shoes, poured three glasses of wine and handed one to Janet.

"Can't wait for tomorrow!" Janet sniffed the glass and took a sip. "Spinsters or not, those girls in the movie certainly had a grand time in Europe. I'm expecting to do the same. Although, I suppose Europe was much prettier back then, before the war."

"I don't think any nation really recovered after the Great War. The movie was made to put a little humor in everyone's lives. Totally Hollywood."

"Ah, but I heard Frenchmen are romantic." Sue hugged her pillow and looked dreamy-eyed out the open window.

Lace curtains rustled gently in the breeze. The cool air felt good. Janet rose and looked out at the stars shining in the night sky. The village was quiet but for a dog barking. No one stirred in the streets.

"This is a nice little town." Janet sipped her wine. "Wouldn't it be nice to live here? Have a little apartment of your own. Wear civilian clothes. Dresses. Yellow, blue, pink! Cute little bows on our shoes. Heels?"

"Gosh, if I could just wear lipstick I'd be happy."

"If only our uniforms weren't uniforms!" Sue tossed the pillow to the foot of the bed. "Army green! Who looks good in Army green?"

"I know. We should be allowed to choose our own colors," Marty agreed.

Janet laughed. "Then we'd look like a parade of Easter eggs!"

"Well the least they could do is design a uniform with some style. Something snazzy. A uniform that a lady looks good in."

"Exactly! How about they get Hollywood to design our uniforms."

"Now there's a plan!" Janet smiled, sipping her wine. They fell silent for a moment, Janet's thoughts going back to her home in Pennsylvania.

"If I lived here, I'd buy all the antique furniture in the shop we went to today," Marty mumbled as she curled up in her bed.

"There were some beautiful pieces. That's for sure." Janet was about to return to her bed when the sky lit up and a flurry of helicopters pulsated overhead.

"What's that?" Sue asked, as the beams of headlamps illuminated the room.

Engines rumbled below in the street and echoed against the flats. The whole of Petworth woke to the noise. Lights came on, people called out in the streets, and a chorus of dogs and roosters sounded throughout the town. Marty peered out over Janet's shoulder.

"What's going on?" Sue asked.

"Field ambulances." Janet's heart beat heavy as she watched the military trucks rumble by. The insignias shone bright in the headlights. "Red Cross. Refrigeration Units. Military trucks."

"My God look how many."

"I can't even imagine what's in the helicopters. We have to go." Janet grabbed her suitcase from under the bed. "They're going to need us." She slipped on her shoes.

"We just got here!" Sue complained.

"Yes, we did, but we're nurses, Sue. And those are the men we're here to nurse!"

Marty and Sue joined Janet, and the three ran down the stairs.

Every hut in the hospital had its lights on. The once-quiet alleys were filled with ambulances, medical buses and officer jeeps. Staff members attempted to make sense of the chaos as patients were unloaded and stretchers were carried from the streets to the wards.

A woman's scream came from one of the nurses already at the trucks. Janet was certain it was Dobi. Major McCall could be heard above the roar of the motors, swearing at the "damn Nazis" for the carnage and damage they did. "Castner!" He turned to face her. "Where the hell have you been? We need a supervisor in 105, pronto!"

"Leave, Sir. We came back early," she began, as she brushed shoulders with a medic.

"Well, don't just stand there! Get your uniform on and get to work." He disappeared into the crowd.

Janet still had her suitcase, and her sweater swung over her arm. There were so many people moving around, headlights shining on the streets coupled with flashlights flickering on and off, she could barely tell where she was. Marty tugged on her arm. "Come on, let's put our things away and get to work."

"Did you see some of these guys? Good Lord, they're tore up." Sue covered her mouth as she walked. Janet understood the tears. Blood-soaked blankets and stretchers were everywhere.

"Don't let the patients see you break down," Janet advised.

"Frost says they sent us the worst."

Motors reverberated, jarring the ground as Janet raced to her hut, dressed quickly and jogged back to the heart of the turmoil, directing the stretcher-bearers where to take the patients. The smell of gasoline seeped from exhaust pipes. The faint moan of wounded soldiers murmured in her ears, a haunting, heartbreaking sound. There seemed no end to the unloading of wounded.

"What about this man?" a medic bearing one end of a stretcher asked.

Janet lifted the tag tied to the patient's wrist. Despite a bandage over his forehead, according to the tab, he had a leg wound. Blood seeped through wraps on his wrists, as well.

"What's your name, soldier?" she asked, checking to make sure there hadn't been a mistake.

"Lou," he panted.

"Morrissey?"

The soldier groaned and shifted violently on the stretcher. "No!" he cried out, tossing his head in panic. "Get out of there! Fire!"

The medic answered for him. "Yeah, Louis Morrissey. France was a nightmare." Headlights from an oncoming vehicle flashed across the medic's face. It was then she saw the distress in his eyes, the sorrow, and the pain. "There are more kinds of wounds than just the ones that make you bleed. This man has them. We all do to some degree," the medic said.

"He needs morphine," Janet said. "Quickly, get him to 105, three huts to your left."

"Janet, I'll take care of things out here," Lieutenant Frost came up behind her and rested his hand on her shoulder. "Show these men where to take this patient. They need you in the ward."

With more patients than there were beds, nurses pushed portable IV units down the aisles and set up temporary cots. Others carried wraps and surgical trays. Janet eyed Doctor Freidman and Doctor Jackson writing feverishly on their clipboards, taking inventory of the men and their wounds. Medics moved about the crowded aisle.

Janet followed the stretcher into the hut. The medics rolled Lou Morrissey onto a cot, and took their stretcher out again, each giving Janet a sorrowful grimace. The patient screamed when Janet removed his blanket to look at his wound. Deeply cut, and wide open, bone showed through. Broken bits of shrapnel littered the flesh surrounding the lesion.

"Dobi!" Janet called, "bring the morphine."

"Dobi's not here," Marty whispered in her ear as she brought the tray.

"What do you mean Dobi's not here? It's her station. Where is she?"

"I saw her," one of the other nurses who had overheard their conversation spoke up. "She ran off. Said she couldn't handle the blood."

Janet rolled her eyes but kept further reaction to herself. These men did not need to hear about a queasy nurse. Not now. She rolled up the soldier's sleeve.

"No!" the soldier grabbed her arm. Sweat dripped off his brow, dried blood encrusted his face where the bandage had leaked, and dirt caked his cheeks. Still, a sense of consciousness remained in his eyes. "No more morphine."

"I'm sorry, sir, you need something to ease the pain."

"It's not the pain that hurts." He squinted, obviously in agony. "I can bear the pain."

"Of course, you can, and this will help." Janet took the Syrette from the tray that Marty brought her, and as Marty rubbed a dash of alcohol on the patient's arm, she prepared the needle.

"No!" He pushed the instrument away. "No!"

Not only did his response puzzle her, but it also made her angry. Janet never had to deal with a man refusing morphine before. "Let us help you," she demanded.

Marty tried to hold his arm still, but he grabbed her apron and upset the tray, sending it and the vial of morphine to the ground.

"Go to Hades with that junk!" His voice turned heads as he flung about on the cot. Even with all the other commotion going on, this man's outbursts threatened to put the whole ward in an uproar.

"Very well!" Janet said with a growl. With fifty patients in the hut, doubled onto temporary bunk beds that Frost and his men had assembled, the nurses were already overburdened. She was in no mood for a fight. "Leave him," she told Marty as she fumbled for the instruments on the floor. "There are too many hurting soldiers here to argue with one as stubborn as he is."

"What should we do with him?" Marty whispered in her ear as they both hunted for roll-away syringes and hypodermic needles.

Janet stood and surveyed the crowded hut. "Put him in the linen closet until the others are settled in." She set the found articles back on the tray and nodded for Marty to move the wheeled cot toward the back. "Louis Morrissey, you'll have to wait your turn for the doctor to see you."

 Chapter 4

Morning Reminder

Janet worked back-to-back shifts that night. With so many new bodies, both wounded and well, moving around in such tight quarters, any orderliness was a miracle. Eventually, patients and staff found their places before dawn. Janet found hers in bed if only for a few hours.

She was awakened by the all too familiar call. "Inspection!"

Given only minutes to rise, dress, and make her bed, she stood at attention when Major McCall made his presence. He sniffed around the room like an old hound dog, tested for dust on every counter, and used his beady eyes to search for whatever kind of flaw he might find. A smirk deformed his face. The silence drew out the visit. His frown made the normal routine of inspection painful.

He left without a word, but only a hesitant salute. Marty breathed heavily once the door was closed.

"I guess we passed!" Sue sighed as she lit the burner to the cook stove and then waved the match to extinguish the flame.

"That's a Mr. Bumble if I ever saw one!" Marty made a face at the door. "The way he treats us you'd think we were orphans good only for a bowl of oatmeal and a whipping!"

"It seems like that sometimes, doesn't it? Well, now that the morning excitement is over–," Janet mumbled, looking over Sue's shoulder to see if the coffee had started perking. "Soon as coffee's done it's time to get back to work."

Once the room filled with the aroma of fresh brew, Sue switched off the propane and poured coffee for each of them. Janet stepped out the door, coffee tin in hand and waited for the others.

"I hope the patients are all asleep," Sue said as they approached 105. "That was worse than last month's chaos. Poor fellas need rest."

Janet waited for the air traffic to drone over their heads before she spoke. "I talked to a medic last night. He said something about St. Lo. Our boys are deep into France, if that's the case."

When Janet reached 105, the room was unusually quiet for being so crowded. Marty served breakfast to some of the GIs that could sit up. Cold cereal and fruit. The others would get IVs. A few of the patients sipped coffee. Three nurses changed bandages and Sue administered plasma to an unconscious soldier.

"How's he doing?" Janet asked, concerned for his welfare, for she hadn't notice the man gaining consciousness since he arrived.

"He's lost a lot of blood."

Janet checked his pulse. "His heartbeat is strong."

"Can you get some clean wraps for him?" Sue asked.

"Of course."

Janet hurried to the linen closet. Once there, her mouth fell open and her heart might as well have stopped. On a cot, which didn't belong in the linen closet, lay the unruly soldier which Marty had moved the night before. Sergeant Louis Morrissey. He still wore battle dust melded with sweat and blood on his face, his bandage caked to his forehead. The blanket draped over his wounded leg trailed on the floor. He wasn't unruly anymore. He slept, or so it seemed. "Oh my gosh," Janet whispered and grabbed enough wraps to bring to Sue. She turned to leave with the full intent of returning immediately.

"Why is this foxhole so clean?" Louis mumbled before she could rush away.

She spun around, hugging the pile of gauze and linens. "Sir, we're not in a foxhole." She took a step closer. "You poor dear. I'm so very sorry. I completely forgot about you. What with all the commotion last night." She bit her lip, knowing no apology could make up for the suffering he must have endured.

"Let me get this to my nurse and I'll take care of you personally. I'm so sorry," she repeated.

"We're out of danger?" his voice trailed. His lips trembled, and his red eyes closed. "Major Howie?"

"Oh heavens," Janet moaned and hurried through the crowded aisle to Sue. "Take these."

"What's wrong? You look like you just saw a ghost?"

"I did! I made a horrible mistake."

"What?"

Sue followed her gaze as Janet looked around the hut for a place— any place— to bring another cot. There was none. The hospital room was filled to its maximum occupancy. Every inch of the ward was lodged with soldiers. "There's a man in the closet," she said.

"What?"

"Last night, he was making a tremendous fuss and I had Marty put him in the closet."

"Oh, good grief." Sue took the bundle from Janet's arms and set it on the bed, surveying the room as well. "There's no place to put him."

"I see that."

"What are we going to do?"

"He didn't get any care last night. Dobi!" Janet scrambled across the room to Lieutenant Dobi, who had returned with fresh linen. "I'll take those. Go find Lieutenant Frost. Quickly! Tell him it's a medical emergency."

"But—"

Janet gave the nurse a scowl and immediately the girl saluted. "Yes ma'am."

Lou had only been awake for a moment when he heard the tanks. Bill tapped him on the arm.

"Let's go."

The night was wet and cold. Wind blew sand and broken remnants of prickly bushes against his face. Mud caked his mouth as he crawled on his belly under the hedge. Thick twisted branches tore his pack and scraped his helmet. He dug at the sand to burrow out from under the bramble, Bill at his heels. When he came to the clearing which overlooked the valley, he saw the source of the threatening rumble. Four tanks chewed up the terrain like giant monsters in heat, heading for the hedgerow—bound to annihilate the allied troops.

Lou pulled off his pack and carefully removed four gammon bombs, placing them on the ground between him and Bill. Already stuffed with explosives, the bags bulged with looming danger. He glanced at the tanks approaching, and then cautiously removed the lids to the grenades. Nodding to Bill, he chose two. Bill took the others.

The moon had not risen. Thick coats of mud smeared on their faces would keep them camouflaged if they stayed low. Lou inched down the hillside, ever mindful of the grenades he so warily carried. One inadvertent move, and they'd both be blown to smithereens. A perilous act of heroism, Lou lived for the adrenaline.

As the tanks roared nearer, he crept until he and Bill were close enough to leap to their feet. They ran toward the visionless machines. Dreadful blocks of steel thundering like armadillos, over the terrain. Lou raced past the first tank onto the next as Bill swung his No. 82 onto the deck above the engine. He immediately sped toward the third tank. Just as Lou tossed his grenade, the first tank exploded. Leapfrogging to the fourth, as the third tank blew, Lou pitched the last bomb, it's ribbon flying in the wind, meticulously releasing the pin as it landed on the deck. Lou zipped away and dodged into the grass, covering his ears as the explosion lit up the night. He could see Bill in the fields dashing for the hedge.

"Good gods! We got them!"

Lou opened his eyes to a cold rag wiping his face. Four white walls penned him in very close quarters, and he smelled the strong odor of antiseptic. The person leaning over him was a woman, but he had no idea of where she came from, or where he was.

"Yes, you did. You got them good."

"Bill got away," he mumbled. "He's okay, I think."

"He is, and you'll be okay, too." A nurse. He could tell by the emblem wrapped around her arm—and she spoke gently. "You're safe here. Although I'm dreadfully sorry about the tight quarters. I honestly didn't mean to leave you in the closet all night. The doctor will be here shortly."

She had the soft touch of a young woman. Her sparkling hazel eyes glistened with color like a crystal-clear pond he'd once seen in the mountains in California. She leaned over him, her warm breath tickled his face. Behind her, a white wall closed them in. The scent of bleach and linen filled his head. Suddenly his heart raced. "Where are we?"

"104th General Hospital, West Sussex England, safe behind allied lines."

He shouldn't be here. He should be in France. "My men? Where are my men? My platoon?"

"Hush," she whispered, as her cool fingers stroked his cheek. "I can't tell you where they are. I can tell you that you've seen the worst. There are brighter days to come. We'll take care of you and we'll come out of this. We'll beat the bloody Nazis and go home."

"Home?" Lou squeezed his eyes shut, and then opened them again. Maybe the image of this woman would fade, and he'd be back where he was supposed to be. Maybe he had been knocked out for a minute. He reached to his head only to discover his hand wrapped thick in bandages. "I was hit." He tried to sit up, but the woman gently pushed him down.

"Yes, and you have a leg injury that needs repair. The doctor will be here in just a moment."

He tried lifting his leg, but all he felt was a pulsating pain in his hip. Part of his body couldn't move, wouldn't move. "Oh god," he whispered. "I'm dying, aren't I?"

"No. But you do need some first aid." She looked over her shoulder. Just then, a door flew open and sunlight flooded the room. So bright was the day, that Lou had to close his eyes.

"What is this man doing in the closet?" The officer blocked the light. Lou opened his eyes again.

"Major, McCall, sir," the woman stood quickly and saluted. Lou felt the need to raise his hand in a salute as well, but his effort was fruitless. No one seemed to notice. The major instead was grimacing at the woman.

"I can explain," she said.

"And you will. In my office. But right now, go and make a bed for him on the floor. Now!"

The woman fled out the door as the major pulled the blanket away, leaving Lou's leg bare. His stare was as intense as if a scalpel had already cut through Lou's flesh. Their eyes met, the major's red with anger. "We'll need to operate immediately. Frost!"

"I'm on it, sir," the doctor behind him said.

Lou jostled on the stretcher as they carted him out of the cramped quarters onto the crowded floor. The tension the major had generated set Lou's heart pounding.

"I don't need this bed," a soldier offered. He held a coffee cup to his lips and nodded a greeting as Lou's stretcher passed by. "He's worse off than I am."

Men and women with hospital aprons surrounded him. The hazel-eyed nurse placed a mask over his face. He smelled ether. He would have struggled, but the first breath he took hijacked his senses. The people fussed over him. Their lips moved, but there were no sounds. The doctor pulled back the blanket from over his leg.

After that, the room faded, and he was back in Normandy, with a few thousand men trudging through mud and bramble.

Clearly death kidnapped his mind, even if it hadn't kidnapped his soul.

Yet.

He could taste it. Smell it. Its flavor had spread over the beaches, picked up by the wind and thrust against his face, his mouth. The taste of dead men's blood on granules of sand filled his body faster than a malignant tumor inching its way through his flesh. Stinging, cutting, pricking him like the thorns of the hedgerow he now scraped against. Death's hunger gnawed at him.

"That's what war's all about, isn't it, Bill? If it isn't about killing, it's about dying." Lou whispered, because no one knew if Germans lurked on the far side of the dirt walls that surrounded them.

"Men have been performing this ritual for ages, Lou. No reason to change things now, I guess. Better to die a hero than live a coward."

Lou gave his friend a nod. The twinkle in Bill's eyes still shone, despite the mud and scars and sweat of battle. His helmet tipped to the side with an attitude that his smile mimicked.

"Wonder how Jack's doing," Lou said, aware of the company's aloneness. Cut off from the rest of the world, it seemed. Surrounded by the enemy that teased them, prowling on the other side of the brush. Attacking only enough to torment them. "They know where we are. They know we're here. I hope Jack's better off than we are."

"We might see him at St. Lo. That's where everyone is supposed to meet up, you know? This marching business is rough. Maybe we should have taken up flying, instead."

"Nah. My heart's on the ground. Had too many dreams of falling."

Bill laughed. "Dead is dead."

Lou curled the wad of saliva under his tongue. No matter how hard he tried, he couldn't rid the foul metallic taste of war. He spat. Most of the guys reeked of fear: pale complexion, sunken eyes, and sweat that dripped off their foreheads. Bill remained mysterious. The man smiled too much to read.

"Ever fear death?" Lou asked him.

"Every day. You?"

"Yeah."

"I remember back home, having a beer and talking about the war."

"Me too," Lou agreed.

"Bar talk's a whole lot different than life," Bill commented. "Sometimes I wonder why I'm here."

Lou glanced over his shoulder, the beach now miles behind them. A long stream of bodies followed them inland. No longer could he see the dead, or hear the surf beating its war cry. But the corpses of the young men who had answered the call still haunted him. Some of the men had been drafted, some of them, like him, had enlisted. Gone now, leaving soon-to-be weeping mothers and distressed wives. Children. The ultimate sacrifice. Someone would have to bring the news. Someone would place folded flags in tear-soaked gloves. Someone would make the coffins, the headstone, the crosses.

"Their lives can't be spent in vain. That's why we move on. The task isn't done," Lou answered.

An explosion sent the GIs tumbling under a cloud of smoke. The lone tank that led the parade keeled on its side. Lou dropped to the ground as the rattle of a machine gun spat a volley of bullets through the hedgerow. He rolled into a ditch and held his breath. Yanking a grenade from his belt, Major Howie held his hand in the air. A signal to wait.

Lou had a good pitching arm, an asset he had developed in high school. He'd been the hero of his senior year, scoring a shutout against Dayton High in their last playoffs. If anyone could annihilate the operator of that MG-42, it'd be him. He just needed to know where to toss the goods.

The major waved to the scout on duty. Lou knew the man. Peter McGillis. A tall, lanky fellow from Pennsylvania. Catholic, like Lou. They'd had a conversation while flying over the Atlantic. Peter had a sweetheart back home, someone not of the faith and he wasn't sure if God took kindly to that sort of relationship.

"God's not all that critical," Lou had consoled him. "Isn't it God that told us to love people? Heck, he even told us to love our enemies, but I don't think he meant the Nazis."

Peter had listened with anxious ears and Lou had taken advantage of the moment. "Men make rules about who to love and who not to love. You know? Men, not God."

Peter had nodded, satisfied with that answer. "I like your reasoning. I'm going to propose to her as soon as I get my first furlough home."

Peter was a good scout. As tall as he was, his feet were light. He had kind of a grace about him that reminded Lou of a gazelle. He never could figure out how someone could walk softly while wearing combat boots. But Peter had it in him. He crept to the edge of the hedgerow, and moved cautiously down the row of thorny bushes, pushing aside the prickly branches with his bayonet, carefully, vigilantly, while the whole company watched and held their breath.

He stopped short, nodding into the brush. He'd found the German.

For his reward, a volley of bullets drummed into Peter's chest. Soldiers yelled, shooting, diving under cover behind boulders, ditches. Lou pulled the pin to the grenade with his teeth, jumped up, and threw. Without waiting for the explosion, he had another potato masher in his hand.

They fought for an hour, perhaps more. No one kept time, but shadows lengthened, and the sky dimmed before gunfire finally ceased. Alive, barely. Exhausted. Despondent, Lou sat in the dirt and leaned against a Hawthorne tree as he watched medics bring the stretchers and carry his men away; his friend from his hometown, and twenty-four other soldiers he'd been assigned to. He knew them all. By name.

So many of his division had died on the beach, and now they were being picked off like grouse in the brush. Not half an hour went by that the troops didn't skirmish with a sniper, or a gunner, or a tank barging through the hedge. They had made little progress since they entered these hedgerows. Too many ambushes. Lou wondered if they'd get to St. Lo on time. Or if they'd get there at all.

He pulled a cigarette from the pack in his pocket. Unable to hold the match steady enough to ignite it with his fingernail, he wondered if this was what a combat breakdown felt like. What should have been sweat dripping down his cheeks appeared to be tears. He wiped his face with his sleeve.

Major Howie stooped next to him and placed a steady hand on his shoulder. The touch did something inside of him. He bit his lip. "Soldiers don't cry," Lou said and locked eyes with the officer. "They march, they fight, they save each other, they die. But they don't cry." He breathed deeply.

"Yes, they do, Sergeant. Every day. We all do." The major offered him a light.

Lou puffed until the embers glowed, and then nodded thanks. The smoke somehow eased the pain inside, like a wool blanket warms the body on a cold night.

"We did something back there that made a difference, Sergeant. We did the impossible." He lit his own cigarette. "It might seem like we failed. We lost a lot of men, but not as many as they expected. And we got in. We're in France now, and we have the Germans running. You watch and see what happens."

"Yeah," Lou answered, thinking of all the men who were slaughtered. Thinking of Peter. Of Peter's girl waiting at home for him.

"Those boys are heroes." Major Howie took a puff off his smoke and patted Lou on the shoulder. "There's no dressing for all the wounds we're suffering, you know that. Except to win this war. Morale is everything, Lou. You tell your men they did good. You tell them we're going to make it to St. Lo and we're going to get Hitler out of France. Believe it in your heart and they'll believe it too, and by God we'll do it."

Major Howie's words comforted him.

Lou fell fast asleep, still unaware of the doctors, the nurse, or the mask over his face.

 Chapter 5

Major Billet

Most of the patients had been cared for quickly, and moved on to the general hospitals inland. With only half the number of soldiers left in orthopedics, Janet had settled into a comfortable routine, exchanging shifts with Marty and Sue in ward 105. She kept the nurses under her charge busy washing sheets, sterilizing equipment, sharpening needles, and running the hospital in an orderly manner. Hard work awarded her restful sleep.

The hospital had been under temporary command of the rigid Major McCall, an older man whom Janet considered heartless. A stickler of regulations. Janet had not, yet, met her commanding officer, Major Billet. The lack of introduction didn't bother her. Lieutenant Frost was readily available for any problem that needed a resolution.

Late one evening after a long day of tending to new patients, Sue jostled her awake. "Get up. Lieutenant Frost wants you!"

"What?" Janet yawned, stretched, and peeked at the clock by her bed. The hands clearly showed zero three-thirty. "Why? I'm not on duty until zero six hundred."

"Don't ask me why. He said it was the major. You'd better get out there, though." With that, Sue slithered into the shadows to undress by her bed.

"Major Billet is back from London?" Janet went through the motions of waking, though her heart wasn't in it. Images of home had filled her dreams just moments before. She could smell the perfume of lilacs by her porch, if only in her imagination. "Dang it, Sue. Just when I was back in Pennsylvania among all the cabbage, corn, and coal fields."

"Not my fault," Sue mumbled. "I'm no boss around here. Let us know what the major's like so I know which perfume scent to wear. I'm not getting a good feeling about this one."

"Me neither, if he's calling at this hour. How was your watch?"

"Boring, as usual. Nothing to do but smoke cigarettes and play solitaire. There are only five men in the ward right now and they're asleep. Men! They're all alike. Doesn't matter what's got into them. Bullets, shrapnel, or attitudes. They still sleep like babies when the lights go out."

"Not all of them evidently," Janet retorted and threw her nightgown at the foot of the bed. "Or I wouldn't be pulled out of bed this early in the morning." She picked up the nightgown and folded it neatly, just in case there was an inspection that morning.

"Don't complain. You didn't have to work with Dobi tonight. I swear that girl is getting downright depressing. She's got the worse attitude. Can't we request a transfer for her?" Sue asked.

"No."

"Did you know she's married?"

Janet gasped. "Dobi?"

"To some English soldier. His folks live in Horsham."

"Where did she ever meet him?"

"She says she used to live here. I don't know. Can't we at least change her shift?"

"No, we can't ask for a different shift for someone else. We don't even get to choose shifts for ourselves."

Sue groaned and sat on the bed.

"Where is Lieutenant Frost?" Janet asked, slipping on her fatigues.

"Somewhere outside."

"I'm not ready for this," Janet grumbled as she pulled her coat from the rack.

"Is anyone, ever?" Sue disrobed as quickly as Janet dressed and buried herself under her blanket. "Don't wake me unless there's coffee and steak and eggs."

"Good grief!" The mirror in front of Janet told her no lies. Sleep still beckoned. Even her hair would not cooperate, but she pinned what ends she could gather into a bun, topped it with her cap and shook her head. "It's useless," she concluded.

"It's dark out," Sue advised. "Frost won't be able to tell what you look like."

"I thought you said the major wanted to see me?"

"Yes, that's what Frost said. That was his excuse, but who knows. Lieutenant Frost is West Sussex' Clark Gable. You're so lucky! I'd give anything to be hitched to a man like him!"

"There's nothing going on between us. You're obsessed with romance, Sue."

"And you aren't? Don't we all dream to be married someday?"

"Of course," Janet whispered. "But not to someone like Lieutenant Frost!" Still gazing at the mirror, she'd forgotten about her own desire to have a family. Would this war make her so tough in the end that she'd forget how to function in civilian life? With all the work ahead of them, when would there be time to get to know anyone? Daily drills, stocking the wards, assigning duties to the seventy-three nurses that were now stationed here, not to mention surgeries and caring for the patients, Sue was crazy to think a romance between anyone on base was possible, much less between her and someone like Lieutenant Frost. Janet gave Sue one last puzzled look, and stepped outside.

Sue's voice faded as Janet shut the door. "Why not?"

The night could not have been darker. The small red tip of a cigarette revealed Lieutenant Frost's whereabouts. He pinched the end with his finger, and then stomped on the embers with his heel.

"What's this? A kidnapping?" Janet asked, her voice a whisper.

"Major Billet sent for you."

"He's back? And now he wants to talk to me at zero dark thirty? I don't even know him."

Lieutenant Frost shrugged his shoulders. "That's his request."

Janet grunted. What kind of officer is this Major Billet? She let Lieutenant Frost lead her through the main alley. None of the huts were lit except for 108, where Marty had night watch over transferable patients who were due to be moved in a few days. Janet had a sneaking suspicion Martina was up late playing cards and smoking cigarettes with the guys. That's what went on in 108.

"Did he tell you why?"

"No."

"Is he angry?"

"I don't believe so. Just the opposite, I think. He's a man of little words, but observes much."

"Well if he just got here, what has he observed? What did I do?"

"I'm not sure. He's been here a few days, I can tell you that much."

The major's office was also his quarters. A brick house at the end of the drive, separated from the huts by a dirt road and a stand of Hawthorne trees. A cobblestone path led up to the porch. Ceramic pots with wilted plants balanced on the railing. A porch swing. Paned windows draped on the interior with lacy curtains.

Lieutenant Frost knocked on the door and stepped back. The light from the porch lamp illuminated a look of worry on his face. She was about to ask him what was wrong when a voice from inside beckoned them.

"Come in!"

Lieutenant Frost opened the door for Janet and followed her inside.

"Thank you, Frost! You're dismissed."

"Yes, sir."

Janet turned around to see him salute the major, excuse himself, and glance sympathetically her way. He took a step back onto the porch and shut the door.

"Come in, Castner." Light from a fireplace flickered, casting a red glow on Major Billet, standing by his desk, and on the walls behind him. Young for an officer, he held his head high and looked down on her with invasive blue eyes. She advanced slowly. A warm and toasty fragrance of wood perfumed the room. Behind the major stood a large grandfather clock, which reminded her the night had passed into morning. Janet blinked the sleep away in disbelief. Zero three hundred hours. What on earth could he possibly want? She silently hoped Lieutenant Frost had not gone far.

"Please!" Major Billet possessed all the glint of someone wide awake. His uniform starched and pressed, the buttons shimmered in the firelight. His eyes fixed on her, his strong jaw cocked in a sort of cunning smile that sent a shiver down her back.

She walked into the room cautiously. He ushered her to a large, cushioned chair. An antique made of etched cherry wood and velvet upholstery.

"Make yourself comfortable."

She couldn't help but give him a cold stare. Comfortable would be back in her own room on her own bed. She sat down. He pulled out a cigar box and offered her a stogie.

"Heavens, no! Thank you," she said. She smoked, but not cigars.

He laughed. "I suppose you're wondering why I had Frost wake you and bring you here."

"Well yes, sir, I am."

"I've been back from London for a while."

"Yes, Lieutenant Frost told me."

"I like to watch my staff without them knowing. I get a better sense of their personalities, their strengths and of course, their weaknesses. Doing so helps me to evaluate their individual performance better. See where discipline is needed. You know?"

He strolled to his desk and picked up a half-emptied bottle of scotch. The golden liquid glistened as he tilted the flask and poured. Swirling and splashing, the alcohol made a grand display as it filled a shot glass. "I couldn't help but notice how skilled you are with the nurses, and in surgery. I did well making you supervisor. Very detailed eye. Very nice."

"Thank you, Sir," Janet whispered, not sure where he was going with this.

"You don't remember me, do you?"

Janet squinted at him, wondering if her mind had failed her. "Remember you?"

"Last year. Fort Mead, Maryland."

She shook her head slowly, having no idea what he was talking about.

"I wasn't a major then. I was a captain." He laughed softly and walked over to her. His hand shook a bit when he offered her the glass. What would she do with a shot of alcohol in her body at this hour in the morning? Her eyes met his and that's when she saw how red they were.

"I recognized your name when I was given the list of new nurses to our unit. I must admit I was thrilled."

She refused the drink.

"I fell in love with you last year, Janet." He downed the whiskey in one gulp and poured another. How could she tell him she didn't remember him after an assertion like that?

"I inspected your barracks once as part of my training. You caught my eye. In fact, I couldn't stop watching you. Your beauty has haunted me ever since. Such grace!" His laugh seemed to mock his words. "You look like the king's daughter, you know? Such a romantic, aren't I? Don't you remember the celebration after your basic training? There was a party on base. I asked you to dance. The band played 'Paper Doll' by the Mills Brothers. Remember?"

Slowly the memory returned to her. Major Billet had been the handsome young captain who had swept her onto the dance floor. She thought the gesture nothing more than a caper. A silly jaunt which she shared with her friends. Dancing with a captain! She never took his attention seriously.

Janet never saw him again after that night. She flew on to Tennessee the next day, leaving the memory behind.

"I'm going to buy a paper doll that I can call my own ... " he sang, and then swallowed another shot. "You didn't know it, but I watched you. Daily. I'm watching you now." He fell into his desk chair and grabbed the bottle. "I'm glad you're here. I've been hoping we would cross paths again. I want you to know that."

"Why?" Janet began, not sure how to put her thoughts into words. "Why did you wake me up to tell me this."

"You'd be getting up anyway. Zero six hundred, correct? Ward 105 this morning."

Worse than a stalker, he would know her every move. She clenched the arm to her chair, restraining herself from running out of the room. "Yes, sir," she said.

He tilted his head. "I called you in here to let you know I want to be friends." He lifted his glass in a toast. "Close friends. Anything you want, anything you need, you just come to me and I'll make it work. We're a team here. Furloughs, leave, anything. Just ask me."

"Yes, sir. Thank you, sir. But ..."

He raised his brow. "But?"

"Isn't that against regulations?"

"Of course, it is, if you're in the States when the country is at peace. But we're not. This is war. Trivial matters are overlooked. We're here to do a job and that's to patch up the wounded men that come in from the front. My job is to look after the staff. To make sure you're ..." his voice tapered and then he smiled. "...well cared for. Your health is just as important as the men who will be coming here. That's my job. Remember that."

"Yes, sir."

He took another slug of whiskey, licked his lips, and looked her square in the eyes. "A man knows what he wants in a woman, Janet. You've been on my heart for over a year. I've never forgotten you. When this war is over ..."

Janet cleared her throat and jumped to her feet. "Sir, it's late. And the war isn't over. So, for now, may I be dismissed? I really do need to get ready for work."

He rose slowly, and sauntered, taking his time to move from behind his desk to where she stood at attention. His blue eyes penetrated her heart. So sad, so longing. So completely pompous! His breath was hot and foul smelling as he leaned near her. "I'm not always like this. I had to drink half a bottle of Scotch to get up the nerve to tell you how I feel about you, and I don't drink. Honest. Not a word to anyone about tonight. That's an order."

"Yes, sir."

"You're dismissed." He managed a salute. "Janet."

She stopped before going outside, turned and glared at him.

"Lieutenant, I meant what I said. Not a word."

She opened her mouth to speak, but what could she say? She saluted, and quickly slipped into the night.

 Chapter 6

Father Dean

Janet attended mass that Sunday. Progressive, by Catholic terms, Father's sermons spoke to the times. Even though he was clearly an advocate for peace, Father Dean never once condemned the war but insisted the Allies had a duty to mankind to stop the atrocities of Hitler. He was never without an encouraging word to both the staff and the patients who came to see him.

After mass, Janet was compelled to confess. The sense of guilt for having left a wounded man in the closet disturbed her sleep. She thanked God that nothing happened to him that night. She also wanted to confide in Father Dean. If anyone could help her with Major Billet, he would be the one. Despite Billet's warnings, Janet did not hesitate to talk about what happened. Pouring her heart out to a priest wasn't disobeying orders.

The chapel was dark when she entered, aside from two low-burning candles on the improvised altar made up of two card tables and a clean white cloth draped over it. She dipped her fingers in the holy water by the door, made the sign of the Cross, and genuflected briefly, catching her breath to calm her racing heart. Confession was not what made her nervous. Goodness, she had been acknowledging her sins and wrongdoings ever since she was a child. However, this was the first time she ever had to make a confession concerning a relationship with a commanding officer. She took a deep breath and strode quietly to the screened-off corner which Father Dean affectionately called Confession Nook.

She thought she heard someone cough at the far end of the Nissen hut, but in the dark, there was no telling if she was alone or not. What did it matter? Many people came to pray. There was so much to ask help for these days.

Janet slipped into the confessional, seated herself in one of the two chairs, and rang the bell. She sensed Father Dean's appearance behind the curtain.

"Let us pray," he said.

When they had finished the ritual of confession, Janet thanked the priest for absolution. "And…" she said, before he left. "And I need to talk to you."

He waited in silence.

"There's a man here. An officer. Someone higher rank than me. He seems to have fallen in love with me."

The silence was deafening, the struggle inside of her unreal.

"He told you this?"

"Yes. I was completely taken aback. I had no idea!"

"Do you love him?"

"No!" That came out louder than she wanted it to. "I'm sorry." She bit her lip and lowered her voice. "I barely know him, but he says he fell in love with me a year ago when I was going through basic training. I hardly remembered him. He's my superior and I'm not sure what to do."

"I see." After a long sigh, Father Dean spoke carefully. "I would suggest you do your duty for which you've been sent. Take each day one at a time, and pray, especially when this officer is near. God will deliver you. I will also pray for the both of you."

"Thank you, Father."

 Chapter 7

Lieutenant Frost

Colonel Jim Wyler had been flown to the hospital by helicopter, along with several other men late at night. No one said anything to Janet about where he'd been fighting or how his wounds came about, but his leg had been nearly severed—the worse she'd seen since she'd been in Sussex.

She was on night shift. There were no other patients in the surgical ward 110 and most everyone in camp was asleep when the choppers arrived. Marty was the nurse anesthetist, and Lieutenant Dobi the attendant. Sue had joined Janet, in case they needed someone else.

Janet and Lieutenant Frost had a rhythm when they worked. Janet and Lieutenant Frost had a rhythm when they worked. Skilled, quiet and talented, Janet knew what he needed and when.

"His bone is shattered." Frost said with a voice that was muted from under his mask. "And there's some infection. We'll have to flush the wound."

Janet prepared the saline solution in a large tub, and gathered a tray of instruments.

He looked over his shoulder to Sue. "Make a note of the infection on his medical record."

"Dobi has the clipboard," Sue responded, glancing around the room. The girl was nowhere to be seen. Having left the clipboard on a table near the door, Sue picked up the document and immediately began writing.

Four stressful hours they worked repairing the colonel's leg, setting bones and sewing together torn tissue. The final instrument was not laid down until almost morning.

"Let's clean up," Frost finally said. "We're done. Leave enough of the wound open to prevent internal infection." He straightened and took off his mask. "Thank you, Lieutenant Alvarez," he said to Marty. "I have to say, all three of you did remarkably well tonight for such a late hour. That was a gruesome wound."

Janet wiped her cheek with her sleeve. "You don't know what a pleasure it is working with you, Lieutenant."

"Like any other doctor, I assume."

Marty laughed, "Don't assume!"

"What do you mean?" Frost scrubbed down, and Janet untied his gown.

"Let's just say there are some doctors that don't show appreciation toward their nurses," Sue said.

"Not that we want any extra credit. We are, after all, just doing our duty." Janet dropped the tools in the enamel basin and poured the alcohol solution over them.

"More than that." An endearing smile greeted her when she looked up at Lieutenant Frost.

"Some of us are just doing our duties," Sue took the opportunity to approach the two. "However, some of us aren't even doing that. You might have noticed the absence of one nurse in particular."

"Where the heck did Dobi go?" Janet asked.

"She couldn't stomach it. Again! She's outside."

"I've talked to her before about leaving during an operation. Guess I need to bring down the hammer!"

"Not now." Frost gently took Janet's arm. "Give yourself a break. We were at the table for four hours. You'll have time to talk to your nurse. Get some rest."

"You're right."

"You haven't had a leave either, have you?"

"A little. We cut our last leave short when the fellas from St. Lo came in. We've gone shopping in Petworth for the day between shifts, but I haven't had a leave yet."

"You should ask for one."

"Maybe." Janet had been avoiding Major Billet, even though Marty and Sue begged her ask for a leave, so she could spend the night in town with them. In fact, Janet said a silent thank you at Mass every Sunday for the Army keeping Major Billet too busy to approach her again. "I will."

"What are you doing tomorrow night?" Lieutenant Frost asked. He folded his apron and wrapped it over his arm.

"I'm baking cookies tomorrow. Seems the staff around here has a sweet tooth. You're welcome to come get your fill or chocolate, too."

"I'd like that."

"How about after my shift tomorrow afternoon? We'll have coffee in 103. There's a kitchen there."

"Excellent!"

He saluted her, and they parted.

Janet peeked into 105 before she retired to her quarters. Still feeling guilty about what she had done to the soldier Morrissey, she wondered about his condition. The last time she saw him he'd been somewhat befuddled from both the anesthetic and war trauma.

The hour was late, and so most everyone was asleep. The nurse on duty dozed on a chair at the table and woke when Janet walked in.

"Can I help you?" she asked.

"I just wanted to see how things were going in here."

"Oh." She rubbed her eyes and yawned. "You're looking at it. Everyone's out for the night. What time is it?"

"Late. We had a long surgery."

"A couple more patients arrived today. A Private Zoey Patterson and a Sergeant Ray Armstrong. They both have multiple injuries. Other than that, things went well. Neither of the new patients needed emergency surgery. Just some clean bandages and some TLC. The doctors will look at them tomorrow."

"That's good. And how is Sergeant Morrissey?" Janet asked.

"Morrissey?" The nurse picked up the clipboard.

"The soldier in bed number eight."

"Oh! Him? He slept most of the day. I managed to feed him a bowl of soup this afternoon, but it took a little coaxing."

"Do you mind if I look to see how he's doing?"

"No, go right ahead," the nurse offered.

Janet walked over to Morrissey's bed. The light in the hut had been turned low so that the soldiers slept in the shadows. Morrissey slumbered peacefully. She felt his head, concerned that he might have developed a fever, but he was cool. When she pulled the blanket over his shoulders and brushed his hair away from his face, he opened his eyes.

"I didn't mean to wake you."

He stared at her for the longest time. "You're the nurse in my dreams."

She laughed. "I hardly think so. I've only just met you."

"No. You were there in that white room. White everywhere. Like heaven. And then there were doctors surrounding me."

"That was hardly a dream. Probably more like a nightmare. I locked you away in our closet for the night to keep you out of trouble."

He smiled meekly. "You put me in a closet?"

"Well, yes. When I and another nurse tried to give you morphine, you imperturbably flipped our tray, spilling all our instruments on the floor. So, you can't say you didn't have it coming." She returned his grin.

"That's what my mother used to say."

"I'm glad you're feeling better."

"Am I?"

Janet laughed. "If you weren't, you wouldn't be talking. You haven't been in a normal state of mind these last few days."

"I was fighting a war."

"I meant since you've been here. In the hospital."

His smile disappeared. "I know what you meant."

As she feared, Sergeant Morrissey suffered from shell shock, tormented by memories that were caged away in his mind. She had seen the same trauma in other patients. "Well, then maybe you can rest from all that hostility, now."

"I'm trying," he assured her. She patted his hand and wiped the curls from his forehead. There was no need to keep him awake any longer.

"Get some sleep."

He nodded, his eyes already closed.

 Chapter 8

A Moonlit Meeting

This was the first night in two weeks that Janet had been able to see the moon. Her impression of British weather along the Channel was less than favorable. At least in Pennsylvania the sun shone sometimes. Not so on this grey and misty coast. Even now, after the rain had stopped, storm clouds passed overhead at a frightening speed. They'd broken enough to let the ominous rays illuminate the path that meandered through the now quiet huts. Soft lights glistened in the windows of the wards, and shadows of the nurses inside on night watch could be seen.

Even though the smell of fresh baked cookies earlier that day had lured the staff to hut 103, it'd been emptied before the sun went down. Now the quiet evening offered more peace than Janet had seen since she came to Petworth.

Lieutenant Frost had been waiting outside for her. He flicked the ashes from his cigarette and pinched it out when she approached. "I could smell your cookies clear across the fields.

If you're not more careful, the Germans will be tracking you down and holding you for ransom."

Janet laughed. "I doubt I have any recipes they don't already own!" she answered. "Come inside."

She lit the propane stove and filled the aluminum coffee pot with water and the basket with grounds while Lieutenant Frost opened the cookie jar on the table. "Gone!" he mumbled and straddled the chair.

"Not all of them. I hid some."

She felt odd, alone with him, as if something romantic was supposed to happen and she wasn't sure she was ready for it. She reached for the hidden cookies and put three on a saucer.

When the room filled with the aroma of fresh brewed coffee, she poured each of them a mug. "Sugar?"

"There's enough sweetness in the room already," he answered all too quickly.

"Well, there's sugar in the cookies. You can dip them in your coffee if you want."

"And get them soggy after you worked so hard to obtain this nice crunchy texture?" He took a bite. "Very good, Janet. Reminds me of home!"

Janet sat across from him. Her mind raced back to her grandfather's farm. "I'd be sitting on the porch swing about now, right in the middle of the cabbage fields, if I were back with my grandpa. Listening to crickets and frogs. Taking care of him," she grew somber, thinking about the last days she spent with her grandfather. As ill as he had been, he still hobbled out on the porch to sit with her. "Where's home for you?" she asked.

"California. For the last five years before I was deployed. At least ..." He looked up, those huge dimples showing off his strong features. "At least, that's where my family lives now."

"By family you mean your parents? Or—"

"My wife."

Well that set things straight right! "How silly of me. Of course, you're married."

"How about you?"

Janet shook her head. "No time. Not with a nursing career. Haven't met Mr. Wonderful yet, either," she answered, relieved in a way that he was married, and she didn't have to worry about impressing him. This was hardly the time or place for a romance. "I bet you miss her!"

"Every day."

"How long have you been away?"

"Three years next month. I went home once at Christmas in '41, that was it."

"You'd think the Army would be a bit more compassionate," she said, hoping she'd have a lighter sentence.

He laughed. "This is war, Janet. The only passion the government has is to win. I spent a year in Northern Ireland with Operation Magnet, building the hospital there. I thought I'd get a furlough in the spring, but instead they sent me to Australia. You..." he paused for a moment and set his cookie carefully on his plate. "You heard about what happened there?"

"You mean when those poor nurses were killed? Yes. I'm afraid that incident sobered the entire medical team I trained with. No one is immune from the atrocities of war, I guess."

"I was working at a station hospital there." He leaned back in his chair and breathed deeply, closing his eyes as he shared the memories. "Those were good people who died. It was like a dark cloud settled all around us after that. No one smiled. The wounded poured in like a flood. We worked fourteen, maybe fifteen hours a day. The sound of an airplane overhead would send panic throughout the camp and we'd keep an eye on the sky for paratroopers. We flinched if there was movement in the brush. No one rested." His eyes locked on to hers then, his voice somber. "The worse part of it all is that there were no victories. Only one defeat after another.. From the way things are going, I'm not certain Australia will recover." He took a sip of his coffee. "So, you see, I consider myself lucky being transferred back here. I much prefer the European Theater to contending with the Japanese."

"Even after the Blitz?"

"London isn't the only target. The Japanese are just as likely to blitz us off the globe. Besides, it's not my own safety I'm worried about. Were I not a doctor, I'd be on the front lines with the rest of our servicemen. No. I'm concerned for the other nurses and our wounded. Our mission is to save lives."

"And the lives in Australia?"

His frown pierced her heart. He seemed to have taken offense. "I consider myself lucky, but I didn't ask to transfer. I would have stayed. My commanding officer felt I was needed here. You've experienced the reason this theater is here, you know? Flushing Hitler out of France is no easy feat."

"Yes. I know."

Frost bit his lip. "We'll be very busy in the next few months." He raised a cup to her and she tapped his with hers in a toast.

"Well?" Sue asked when Janet snuck back into the nurse's quarters.

"Well what?" Janet knew full well what Sue was asking. She just wanted to make her say it.

"What's he like?" Marty rested her book on her lap. "Clark Gable? Or more like Humphrey Bogart? Surely he swept you off your feet and took you away on a flying chariot to some wonderland over the moon?"

"He's a charming man."

Before Janet could say anything else, Sue broke in with, "Somehow I hear bells. They say Father Dean is a marrying kind of priest."

"Stop it already!" Janet insisted. "We had coffee and cookies and talked. That's it! And if you must know, Lieutenant Frost is married. So, there are no wedding bells which haven't already sounded. For him."

Immediately, a chorus of disappointment filled the room.

"Well that's disheartening," Sue concluded.

"Don't worry. There are plenty of good looking men in the service. And marriage is not the reason I joined." Janet sat on her bed and slipped off her shoes.

"No? Why not?" Sue asked, winking when Janet glanced at her.

"We're just teasing, Janet." Marty lay back on her bed and opened her book. "Although it would be nice to have something to talk about other than broken bones, shrapnel, and bloody towels. A hot romance in ward 105 would fit the bill."

"Or 108," Sue suggested, giving Marty a teasing eye.

 Chapter 9

Cookies

Funny how the grain in wood seems so much more pronounced when it is wet, Janet thought as she stared at the aged, oak door, ignoring the bronze clapper and pretending the cold brass handle was nowhere near her hand. If she acknowledged that the door was made to open, she'd have to enter, and she wasn't certain just what Major Billet had summoned her for. Nor did she have any desire to stand in front of him. Alone. Again.

But orders were orders, and so she took a deep breath and knocked.

"Come in."

Janet opened the door slowly and stepped inside.

"Castner!" The major did not pull his gaze from the papers on his desk, but rather shuffled through them, as though Janet's presence meant little more than a local messenger boy dropping off a memo.

"You wanted to see me, sir?"

He didn't respond. He didn't even act as though he had heard her. She spoke loudly enough, and they were the only two people in a quiet room. No activity outside interrupted the silence; no aircraft, no vehicles.

"Sir?" What game was he playing? The breeze rustled the curtain, letting daylight blink across the window sill. She shifted her weight.

He looked up. "Yes?"

He stacked his papers neatly on top of one another, picked them up, and tapped them on the desk so that the corners were straight and orderly. After setting them into his drawer, he stood. "I hear you make cookies."

Surprised, she stared at him, her mouth agape. "Who told you?"

"Oh, come now, the whole camp raved about your baking. Stirred up a bit of jealousy in the mess hall."

"I'm sorry, sir."

"I hear you also entertained a certain lieutenant with midnight snacks. Cookies, I presume?"

"Sir?"

"Frost, was it?"

"I—"

"Was that all you offered him?"

How dare he! "Sir!"

"I'm not sure what you see in him that you don't see in me. We're both good looking. We're both officers, although I hold rank well over him." He raised a finger. "Ah! Another difference is, Frost has a wife. Or did you know that?"

"I'm aware and I didn't do anything to —"

He held up his hand. "I'm sure you didn't. An upright Catholic girl as yourself wouldn't think of jeopardizing a man's marriage."

She felt the heat rise. "What does my faith have to do with this?"

He interrupted her, a dark shadow fell across his face. "When I give you an order, I expect you to obey it, Lieutenant."

Janet shifted her weight again, straightening her back. His insults were detestable. "I did obey you, sir."

"Did you?" He drew so near that his breath blew her hair and tickled her ears. She scowled and stepped back. "I expected you to keep your mouth shut. Meaning you were not to tell anyone. Not even a priest."

"Sir!"

Had Father Dean told him what she had confessed? Or had there been someone else in that room after all? Was Major Billet commissioning people to spy on her? Dare she ask?

"With all due respect, sir, my confession time is between me and God."

"And whoever else is in the room, I might remind you. The chapel here is not as private as what you're used to back in the States. You should have used caution. Nothing you do here will go unnoticed, Janet," he whispered, though it was more a hiss. "Not if you aren't careful. I was completely transparent with you and I expect you to respect me for it. I need you to."

"Is that all, sir?"

"Isn't that enough? You've humiliated me. I hope your satisfied!"

Janet wanted nothing more than to be gone from him. He didn't let her. He stood between her and the door, his body a bastion imprisoning her in his den.

"I understand. You don't want me to say anything about fraternizing, nor about persuasion, nor inappropriate behavior," she suggested.

"Exactly," he said. "You know any of those infringements are punishable by court-martial. I have no intention of hurting you. You can return the favor."

Janet swallowed and waited, feverish and certain that she must be glowing as red as a lobster from the anger welling inside of her. Why did he put her in this position?

Fortunately, he stepped away before she burst.

"How I wish I could soften your heart toward me," he said. "If only you'd…" He brushed his hair back with his hands and walked to the window. "If only you'd trust me. Ask me for something. Let me help you. Let me be involved with your life."

Janet gawked at him. Oh, the woes of unrequited love, she thought. Never had she expected to play the part of Dulcinea to a Major Don Quixote.

"You're dismissed." He gave her a halfhearted salute and an annoying pout. Janet beelined for the door.

Where the Yellow Violets Grow

 Chapter 10

Tell me

The ground trembled as a fleet of bombers soared overhead. The steady rumble shook her bed. Janet opened her eyes, her heart raced and didn't slow until the aircrafts' roar dissipated into the steady pounding of rain on the roof. A chill rushed into the room when Marty came inside. The night was dark behind her.

"That's the British," Marty clarified when Janet sat up. "And there's another convoy of wounded coming in." She stomped the mud from her shoes, and hung a dripping wet coat on the peg by the door.

Janet put on her coat and reached over to turn on the light.

"We're on blackout," Marty cautioned her.

"Oh great!" Sue exclaimed, tying her blond hair in a ponytail. "More operations by flashlight. You'd think this was the American Civil war what with the conditions we have to work in."

"They didn't have flashlights during the Civil War, did they?" Marty asked.

"There are jeeps out there driving around with no headlamps. Let's get our wounded inside." Janet scurried her friends out the door.

"Where are they taking them? There's no room in 105," Sue said, wrapping her cape over her shoulder.

"McCall moved some patients out of 105." Marty answered.

"Great!" Janet snickered. "Who, I wonder." She grabbed a flashlight on her way out the door. Martina stopped her.

"No lights outside. At all."

"Is there a moon?"

"A sliver of one. Get your owl-eyes on."

Several ambulances lined the alleyway, dark and ominous, the vehicles were all but camouflaged by the night. Sound had been muted as well. Soldiers moved quietly, no one spoke above a whisper as they rushed the stretchers to the Nissen huts. Whatever sounds were made were soon drowned out by bombers flying overhead.

Those who could slip into the shadows did so. Others fell to the ground and froze. Janet hid in the shadow of the dark side of the ambulance and waited. Flashing lights lit up the sky in the distance, toward London—spotlights searching the cloudy heavens for the enemy. When the immediate threat was over, Janet slipped into the ward. Lieutenant Frost stood by the bed of one of the three patients who had just been brought in. Nurses in the room had shut the blinds, but the one nearest Janet remained open.

"What the hell is going on?" someone called from one of the beds in the shadows.

"Who's that?" Janet spoked softly.

"Sergeant Zoey Patterson, I believe." Frost spoke as quietly as she had. "Hip and head injury."

"Ain't no more room in here for strangers!" the man said.

Lieutenant Frost merely glanced toward the dark corner where the complaint came from.

"You! Nurse! Close those shutters! Can't you see the enemy's out there? You're going to get us all killed!" Zoey commanded.

Janet wasn't new to combat-stressed patients, or even unruly ones. She thought little of the soldier's attitude. Maybe all the noise woke him up and he had a recall of combat trauma. She exchanged a smile with Frost and then quietly shut the blinds. Staff had been advised not to provoke patients, so neither she nor Frost said anything. The man eventually went to sleep.

Janet took temperatures of the new patients, changed their dressings, and recorded their vitals in her logbook. None of the new arrivals needed emergency attention, so she made the three men as comfortable as she could and bedded them down for the night.

Once silence shrouded the ward again, Janet put another log in the barrel stove, collapsed on a chair near Frost and listened to the drumming of rain on the roof.

"Fire burns the same wherever you are, you know?" she said, eyeing the occupied beds that surrounded them. Patients who nestled under woolen blankets gave the appearance of peace. A serenity which wouldn't last. Some of these soldiers would be sent back to their units and fight again. Some of them would be sent to more efficient hospitals in the States. Some of them would be discharged and go home to see their families. They were the lucky ones. "There's no difference how the fire burns. Not here, at home, or in campfires that the soldiers make in the trenches in France. Always hot and red and crackling."

The lieutenant straddled his folding chair and handed her a shot glass which he filled with whiskey from his flask. The golden liquid warmed her insides and settled her nerves. "Fire hisses and spits, as if nothing out of the ordinary is going on. The same flame, the same smoke. Just like it did on grandpa's farm when the winters were cold, and snow blanketed the ground. At our finger tips to warm, comfort, or destroy us." She listened to the quiet pop of wood in the fireplace, the rain on the roof, the murmured snore of a soldier. "Half a year has come and gone since I came to Petworth."

"Homesick?" Lieutenant Frost asked and before she had time to answer, he added, "Me too. Sometimes I think I'd have been happier on a farm," Frost said.

"I lived with my grandfather in Pennsylvania and nursed him through his last days. I miss grandpa. I miss my family."

"I'm sorry," he offered.

"Thanks. I guess I'm just feeling melancholy tonight."

"Why's that?"

Janet glanced at Morrissey's bed. "I've been making some avoidable mistakes. I should know better."

"You mean putting the patient in the closet?" he laughed. "There was a lot going on that night. If Major Billet doesn't understand, just tell him I told you to put him in the closet."

She laughed. "I can't do that. Anyway, that's not the problem, I don't think."

"Well if it is, tell him it was my decision."

"Major McCall knows you weren't in the ward, and I'm sure he's told Major Billet everything. Anyway, how could I put you in jeopardy like that? You're long due for a promotion, aren't you?"

"Should be."

"You deserve one."

He shrugged. "If it's up to Major Billet, I won't ever get one."

She frowned and watched him reach in his shirt pocket and pull out a cigarette. He offered her one, which she refused.

He lit his, taking long drawn out puffs. The smoke shone blue and swirled in lengthy streams, which drifted into the dark room.

"What does Major Billet have against you?"

He shook his head. "I don't know."

The way he slumped over, blew out the smoke, and avoided looking at her told Janet otherwise. "Is it because of me?"

When he didn't answer, Janet's blood boiled. "Of all the gall! What did he say to you?"

Lieutenant Frost tossed his half-burned cigarette into the fire. "He thinks we're having some sort of an affair."

"What a troublemaker!"

"I love my wife. I would never do anything to compromise our marriage."

"He's trying to call up the devil!"

"Did he say something to you?"

The story of what happened during her confrontation with the major tottered on the tip of her tongue, but she feared the consequences. "He said plenty, but I'm not supposed to tell anyone."

"Then don't."

"Well, that's not fair."

"Maybe not. Neither is war."

She said nothing more. Frost rose and walked to Morrissey's bed. The patient's eyes were closed, his body relaxed, still in a deep sleep. "I dug an exceptional amount of bone fragment and shrapnel out of him the other day. Make sure that wound stays open, so it heals from the inside out. There's pronounced risk of infection if it doesn't."

"Preventing infection is my forte."

"You'll need to pay extra attention to this one." He looked at her. "I have confidence in you, Castner. It's been a hard couple of nights. Let's go to the officer's dance this month."

"Major Billet will see us."

"Good! I'm not walking on eggshells around him. I have nothing to hide."

"I like your attitude, Lieutenant! Let's do it!"

He smiled. "So, if you'll excuse me, I'm off duty and need sleep."

"Indeed, you do. It's always a pleasure to work with you."

He patted her on the shoulder, gathered his instruments, and left her to night watch.

With the overhead lamp out, and only a few candles flickering in the room, Janet wished she could sleep as well. She yawned and stretched, having half a mind to run back to her quarters and make some coffee.

"Tired?"

Surprised, Janet started at the sound of Morrissey's voice. "You aren't asleep!"

"No, I'm not and I heard every word you two said." The candlelight caught the twinkle in his eyes.

"You're feeling better?"

"I'm more conscious if that's what you mean. My leg is killing me. My arms ache. Your drugs seem to be a temporary fix is all."

"Yes, well, we have to use them sparingly there are so many of you coming to visit."

"I'd be happy with a shot of whiskey, if that's allowed."

"Maybe tomorrow, after that anesthesia wears off." When he pouted, she laughed. "Sorry, soldier. Your health is our number one concern."

"Not my comfort?" He winked at her, the sparkle in his green eyes returned. All cleaned up, he was a good-looking man. "I'll be looking forward to tomorrow. Especially since you've been ordered to pay extra attention to me."

She flushed and stuttered for a comeback. "You heard that too, did you?"

"As soon as the doc said it, healing traveled up my spine. What better medicine than the care of a pretty nurse?"

With a sudden urge to busy herself, she took his arm and touched his vein, checked her watch, and counted his pulse.

"I'm sure it's going faster than normal," he whispered. "What with your touch and all—"

"Stop that. Your heart is beating just fine."

"I didn't mean to embarrass you. Forgive me. Please."

"You didn't embarrass me." She gave him a flirtatious grin. If he only knew how innocent his remarks were compared to the grinding demands of her commanding officer.

"Talking to you helps, you know? I need to be rooted into reality." He closed his eyes, the jovial smile suddenly gone. "Be thankful you weren't there."

"The battles in France must have been terrible," she said, hoping he'd tell her more. Patients who talked about their experiences healed so much faster than those who didn't.

"Normandy was ruinous. So many dead! So many! After the slaughter, we hiked along the hedgerows and were picked off and run over and bombed and—" He stopped, took a breath and wet his parched lips. "We made it to St. Lo. Most of us. Some of us. Major Howie didn't." He grew silent and stared at her, as though he saw someone else instead. "God knows how, but we got there."

She wiped his hair back from his face.

"After our troops bombed the city, there was pretty much nothing left. Snipers. Some Krauts throwing grenades—that's what got Major Howie. He kept talking about what he'd do when we got there. How we'd celebrate. He was going to buy us all a round of the best French vino we could find. He was looking forward to it. But he never made it. After that last blast, we found his remains. There wasn't any room in the ambulance for dead men, not with all the wounded guys, so we put Major Howie on the hood of the lead jeep. He was the first American soldier into St. Lo. That's what he wanted, and by God, that's what we gave him. We carried him up the rubble of St. Lo Cathedral and draped our Colors over him. Me and some of the other fellas said a prayer. A lot of us shed tears. He was deserving of tears. He was a good man. The best major I ever had. Won't be another like him, not in a long time. A born leader." He considered her eyes, a glint of hope in his. "You should have met him. What's your name?"

"Lieutenant Castner."

"First?"

"Janet."

"May I? Call you Janet, that is?"

"I guess," she answered. "I mean, not in front of an officer."

"Yeah, I know." He closed his eyes for a moment, and then continued his story. "You should have met him, Janet. He knew how to life a guy's spirits. That's not an easy thing to do when everybody you know is getting shot at and killed and mutilated."

"I've seen some of those wounds, soldier," Janet assured him.

"He brought me out of the pits when I was ready to give up." Lou blinked tears away as he spoke. "God, St. Lo! So many civilians. Everywhere. Women, boys, little girls strewn across the streets. So much blood staining the rubble you couldn't even tell where it came from. Baby buggies burned, their wheels still smoking with little bodies inside of them, charred. For miles. After we got the Germans out, we stumbled all over the city, looking for civilian survivors. We thought the allies had dropped fliers warning the French, but the wind must have blown them away because we found the leaflets meant for St. Lo scattered across the fields halfway to Paris. Those poor people never saw a one. They didn't know we were coming."

"How devastating!"

"Devastating? Yes." Their eyes met. Sweat beaded on his forehead.

She'd seen that symptom of anguish so many times—fever caused by trauma. If only she could take the pain away. Why had she been so cruel as to put him in a closet? Or to talk to him so roughly. "I'm sorry."

Maybe she couldn't relieve his pain, but she could at least cool his fever. She poured water into a basin and soaked a clean cloth. When the rag absorbed the moisture, she dabbed his forehead. He watched her, his eyes following her every move.

With firelight flickering in the quiet room, the rain, the candles, and the late hour of night reminded her of the long hours back in Corsica, Pennsylvania that she spent nursing her grandfather. All the prayers, all the tending to his illness. All her efforts and she still couldn't save him. She'd make up for that failure, now. "We'll fix you up soldier," she whispered.

"Lou," he said. "Call me Lou."

He had the most captivating eyes. No one had pure green eyes like his. Wide and brilliant, despite his despondency.

"Lou," she said softly, hoping her voice would bring the comfort he needed.

Instead, his smile comforted her.

 Chapter 11

Dobi

Just as Janet was about to enter the ward the next morning, she met Lieutenant Dobi and another nurse rolling a load of laundry out the door.

"Dobi, I've been meaning to talk to you."

Dobi stopped abruptly and saluted. "Yes, ma'am," the lieutenant answered.

"After your shift."

"Yes, ma'am. What's it about?" Dobi boldly inquired.

"Inappropriate behavior during an operation."

"Oh." Her dark eyebrows furrowed, and a pained expression crossed her face.

"We needed you in surgery the other day, and you weren't there. In fact, I haven't seen you in any surgeries. If Major Billet found out …"

The girl's face turned beet red. "You're going to tell Major Billet?"

Sue nudged Janet and nodded to a figure walking toward them. Who else but the major strode down the alley, his dark coat and shiny boots giving him a regal appearance in dawn's light.

"This isn't the time nor the place to discuss it. Come see me after your shift."

"Yes, ma'am."

Janet wished the two nurses would move quicker out of the doorway so that she could disappear inside, but the laundry bag was heavy, and the rollers hung up on the threshold. Major Billet was near upon them and he was the last person Janet wanted to see. Ever.

"Castner!"

Sue stood erect immediately, but it took Janet a moment to turn and salute. Without any more trouble, Dobi and the other lieutenant rolled the laundry to the road and were soon out of sight. The major returned the formality as though it were a bother. "I would like to speak with you for a moment. Follow me."

"Sir?" Janet hesitated to leave her duties. Many of the patients needed dressings. She watched Sue slide into the hut.

"I've got this, Janet," Sue assured her.

"We'll only be a moment," the major said.

The sun had just topped the horizon, casting a golden hue across the fields and reflecting brilliantly on the metal rooftops. Janet squinted as she followed the major, shielding her eyes from the shine, and nearly bumped into him when he pivoted around to face her. "I'm sorry I was so hard about your confession to the priest."

Janet didn't know what to say, so she just stared at him.

"I'm also sorry that your first leave was interrupted. Major McCall informed me that you came back from town on your own. If I had known, I would have acted more quickly in getting you another. I find your actions commendable. You didn't have to cut your leave short, nor did you need to return before your leave was over. Doing so was not a requirement."

"I'm here for the soldiers, not for vacation," Janet admitted.

"You're industrious and loyal. I like that in a soldier. In a woman," he added quietly and stopped to face her.

She shifted her weight and looked away.

"Have you had any time off?"

"No, sir."

"Well, I'm going to put in another request for you."

"Thank you," Janet said, avoiding his eyes.

"The request won't be approved for a little while. There's too much activity going on across the Channel. When things die down, which they will."

"We have no way of knowing, that, sir."

"We've taken St. Lo. The city belongs to the allies. We're gaining ground."

"I hope so. I'm sure that's classified information?"

He shook his head. "Maybe for the public. Not for you. I'll tell you anything you want to know."

Janet fixed her gaze on the trail that meandered through the grassy field to Petworth. What could she do to stop his unremitting and illegal favors?

"How serious are you?"

His question took her by surprise. She faced him. "What?"

"About Frost?"

Not again! She rolled her eyes. "He's a nice guy. We work together. He's a good surgeon. I have no idea what you're talking about when you ask me how serious I am about Frost."

"I need to stay on top of my soldiers' social behaviors. It's my job. I need to know what's going on in my division. We have rules, you know. Protocol. I have a job to do to keep the unit running smoothly."

"There are no procedures at risk. Nothing is going on. Sir."

"You'll be getting your silver bar soon."

"Sir?"

"You can call me Horace."

"Major Billet, I appreciate that you want to give me things. Thank you."

"A promotion isn't a gift, Janet. You've earned it."

She took a chance to look in his eyes and regretted it. He wanted her affection to the point of recklessness. She had no feelings for him whatsoever. In fact, the intensity of his presence made her want to run away. "May I return to work, please? There are men suffering."

"Yes. There are," he snickered.

If she didn't get away soon she'd gag.

"You're dismissed," he offered.

She gave him a quick salute and walked away as quickly as she could. Once past the row of huts, without looking back she broke into a run. There were patients to care for.

Walking into hospital ward 105 wasn't the pleasant getaway from Major Billet that Janet had expected. Sue had her hands full with Zoey Patterson, the sergeant with the attitude. Zoey had a head wound but also had been shot in the hip, which is why he ended up being treated in the orthopedic ward. He wore gauze wrapped over his forehead and walked with a pronounced limp. The kid was prone to temper tantrums. A young, mouthy sergeant.

When she opened the ward's door, Janet unexpectedly promenaded into a battle of words—none of which were clean—and articles of clothing catapulted around the room. She ducked when a pillow flew past her head.

"What's going on here?" Janet had Sue's attention, but three men continued to holler at one another, Zoey being one of them. The sergeant's face burned red with anger while two other patients cursed at him simultaneously.

Lou sat on his bed, his hair disheveled with a stunned expression on his face as though he had just been woken up.

"I give up," Sue said, throwing her arms in the air.

Janet put two fingers to her mouth and whistled loud and hard. Zoey's combatants ceased their assault, but Zoey gave Janet little attention, using the silence as a platform to air his curses.

"Attention, soldier!" Janet pointed at Zoey. He kept ranting.

"Stop!" Sergeant Morrissey's voice resonated, and with an air of authority that brought the argument to a standstill. "You will listen to your superior officer! As a Technical Sergeant, I am your superior, am I not? Sergeant Patterson?"

Zoey clammed up.

"These nurses are both Lieutenants in the same United States military as you. If they tell you to be quiet, then you had better pull up your britches and stuff your mouth with cotton balls, or you'll be facing disciplinary actions."

Fury flushed his face, but Zoey said nothing more. Rather, he rolled back under his covers. Curious as to what the commotion was about, Janet made a note to ask Sue later in the privacy of their room. Inquiring now would possibly trigger another round of fire.

Silence pervaded a long while passed before tempers calmed. Janet and Sue both made the rounds, checking vitals, dressing wounds, and taking temperatures. Sue sat on the bed of one of the patients who had been arguing with Zoey, and talked to him, but Janet was unable to hear their conversation. When it was Zoey's turn for her to take his pulse, he sealed himself further under the covers.

"Come on. I need your arm." Janet pulled the covers back, grabbed his wrist, and took his pulse.

"Let me change that wrap on your head."

"I don't want you touching me," he said. "Have Lieutenant Frost do it when he comes in."

She could have argued with him or demanded her way, but because Zoey was so upset, she thought perhaps it would be better to relent. "Very well," she said, and left his bedside.

"Thanks for setting things in order," Janet whispered to Lou as she read his pulse.

"The man's trouble," Lou told her. "He's not right in his head. He needs to get out of this ward."

"I'll get someone from the NP to examine him."

"Good. He's dangerous."

Later in the day when her shift was over, Janet returned to her hut to make coffee.

Sunlight streamed in from the window, shining on Marty as she twisted her shiny black hair into one sweeping curl and fastened it with bobby pins to fit neatly under her cap.

Sue opened the door flooding the hut with even more bright day.

"Can you believe that sun? Where did that come from?" Janet asked.

"I think the recruits brought it in from L.A. You heard about the new staff arriving last night, didn't you?" Sue stepped outside.

"Oh cripe! I forgot. Does that mean Major Billet is leaving?"

"Not that I heard. Why?"

"Oh, I don't know. Just a wishful thought. Which reminds me, I have to talk to Dobi this afternoon."

"Speak of the devil. Here she comes."

"Grab her. Don't let her get away!"

Janet had already poured a steaming cup of coffee when Lieutenant Dobi stepped inside. The young woman saluted and stood stiffly, as if she were a child about to receive a whipping.

"At ease." Janet offered Dobi a chair near the center of the room and pulled one up across from her. "What's the problem, Lieutenant? Why did you leave this time?"

"Ma'am I was feeling ill that night," Dobi began, fidgeting with the hem of her shirt.

Janet raised her hand to stop her excuses. "That night? What about every night there's work to do? Do you feel ill every time there's an operation in progress? Every time a soldier comes into the ward with a bloody wound? Since when does a nurse have the privilege to feel sick when they see blood? You went through training. Breathe through your mouth and if you must get a breath of fresh air, then do so but good heavens, child, come back! We need you. The patient needs you."

?"

Tears welled in Dobi's already red eyes. "Training wasn't the same as this. There weren't men screaming and carrying on like they do here. And we had a decent room to stay in, showers, and running water. We weren't all packed together with bombers flying overhead."

"So that's it? You can't handle the workload?"

"No, I mean it's part of it, but I'm really upset right now."

"And you don't think anyone else is?"

Dobi rubbed her eyes and then burst out in tears, gurgling some unintelligible sounds as she covered her face with both hands. Janet wanted to slap her into reality, but instead she waited for the lieutenant to catch her breath.

"I can't take it any longer. My husband is twenty-five miles up the road and the Army won't let me see him. They won't give me a leave, and I've been here working my tail off."

Janet sat back in her chair, crossed her arms, and let the woman go on.

"He's wounded, and I don't know how bad he's hurt."

"He wrote you?"

"Once." She wiped her eyes and sniveled. "The letter was not encouraging, either. Like maybe he went blind or something, because he said it was hard for him to see the paper he was writing on. I keep seeing him in every wounded soldier that comes here. I get sick to my stomach thinking that's what my Joey is going through."

"I see." Of course, the woman's story touched Janet's soft spot. Dobi should be able to see her wounded husband, but the Army was such a heartless machine sometimes. "Would it help if I put in for a leave for you?" Perhaps Dobi would work better if she knew how her husband fared.

Dobi nodded, sobbing.

Janet handed her a tissue. "All right then. I'll see what I can do. But you must promise me, until this leave comes through, that you're going to toughen up. No more fainting or walking out of surgery and not coming back. Do you understand?"

"Yes, ma'am," Dobi answered, forcing a smile through her tears.

"These men need us. Your husband isn't the only man wounded from this war. And you made a commitment when you signed up with the Army."

"I'll make myself handle it. Thank you," she said.

"You're welcome. You're dismissed." Janet escorted Dobi to the door. The woman jogged out of sight, still weeping, but hopefully from tears of joy. When she was gone, Sue offered Janet a cigarette and a light.

"You think you can get her a leave?" Sue asked. "She's only been here a couple of months, and there's a pecking order for papers."

"I think so," Janet answered.

"Good luck. By the way, there's a couple of guys in 105 ready to be transferred to another ward. Looks like we might have some breathing space in there again. Now if only Zoey Patterson would get better!"

"If only!" Janet agreed.

"Marty and I are going into town this morning. Thought we'd get some tuna fish so you can make us a tuna-noodle casserole tonight. How does that sound?"

Janet laughed. "How kind. Just don't tell Major Billet I'm competing with the mess hall again. I've already gotten in hot water for that."

"Don't worry, we won't. We don't want anyone else to know how good a cook you are," Sue assured her.

After they left, Janet crawled under the covers in hope for sleep. She still hadn't recuperated from all the double shifts the week before. As soon as she hit the straw mattress, she was out and didn't wake again until early evening when Marty and Sue returned.

"You won't believe what happened!" Sue didn't seem to care if Janet were asleep or not. She sat down at the foot of her bed. The sound of a newspaper netted Janet's attention.

"What's going on with the outside world?" Janet asked.

"There was an attempt to murder Hitler. By his own men."

"Are you serious?"

"Read for yourself."

Stunned, Janet examined the headlines. *"German Generals Reported Leading Open Revolt Against Hitler's Nazis.* Whoa, Nelly! That's unbelievable."

"Too bad they weren't successful," Sue mumbled.

"What happens now?" Marty asked. "I mean, now that we know not all of Germany is behind Hitler, what happens?"

"I guess maybe it means the Allies are a little closer to victory?"

"Hopefully. So, what happens next is we fix up our boys just like we did yesterday," Janet responded. "They're still killing each other out there."

"Okay. Until we're ready to do that tonight, Janet, here is a box of noodles, cheese, and an onion that I stole from the mess hall, and—" Sue held up two cans of tuna fish. "Dinner!"

"No booze." Marty added. "Petworth is clean out for now. Probably because of the officers' dance. Someone went into town and bought all the alcohol. Not until we free France will we get any good wine."

"Oh well, this dinner will be good without booze." Janet rose from her bed and washed, ready for a decent hot meal.

"Delicious!" Sue leaned back in her chair and rubbed her tummy. "So glad I have you for a friend!"

Janet dabbed her lips with a napkin and set her fork on the table. "You'll have to excuse me, ladies. I'm ducking out early tonight."

Marty glanced at her watch. "You aren't on duty for another hour and a half."

"I have some important business to take care of." Tucking stray curls under her cap, Janet reached for her cape and walked out the door.

Hospital staff congregated in the mess hall two roads down from her barracks. The nurses who were still on day shift fed their patients in the wards, so very few people were outside. As Janet strolled down the narrow street, the aroma of boiled lamb, cabbage and potatoes saturated the air so thoroughly she could almost taste it.

The long shadows cast by the setting sun reminded her of home. In the distance, rooftops silhouetted against the fading daylight, and the palatial home of Lord Lech Enfield beyond the city nestled neatly against a field of green. If only the British would let the U.S. Army use the abandoned mansion as their hospital, they'd have a more sanitary set-up than these cramped and dirty Nissen huts.

Major Billet preferred to eat alone. Every evening at sunset he could be seen carrying his dinner in a covered tin plate, coffee cup in hand, to his house at the end of the row. There was no reason that today would be any different.

Stepping briskly up to his porch, Janet rapped on the door. Today she would not be intimidated. Today she would play the upper hand. When she heard him call from the den, she let herself inside. He nearly tipped over his plate when he jumped out of his chair. Janet saluted.

"Castner!" he said, and returned the salute.

"Major, sir," she answered.

"What a surprise. Would you care to join me? I was just sitting down to eat."

"No thank you, sir. I've had my dinner. I'm sorry to interrupt you, but as I'm on night duty and you're so busy during the day—"

"Don't apologize. You know I'm always happy to see you. Please, sit."

She accepted his hospitality and nestled in the cushioned chair across from his desk. "Thank you."

"Care for some Scotch?"

Her eyes lit up. "Why yes, thank you."

He handed her a glass and poured from a freshly opened bottle of Johnnie Walker Red Label. "Straight? Or would you like it Churchill style?"

"Mr. Churchill's recipe works well for me."

He poured some water into the cup, twirled the glass, and then offered it to her. Unlike the last time she visited, his hand was steady, his eyes cheerful, and his welcome warm.

"What brings you to my abode? I feel I should apologize again for the last visit. I was upset." He took his seat. With hungry eyes, he gazed at his food, but instead of picking up his fork, he folded his hands.

"I'm fine with pretending that visit didn't happen." Butter is always a good idea at the dinner table, she thought. "Go ahead and eat. I don't want to disturb your supper. I'll only be a minute." She sipped on the Scotch hoping it would help her form the right words.

"Very well. I haven't eaten since noon."

"That's fine." She watched him cut his meat and take a bite. He pushed a measure of mashed potatoes onto his fork with his knife and put that, too in his mouth while still chewing his lamb. He looked up at her.

She smiled and took another healthy sip of the scotch. Her nerves were settled enough to begin. "You said you wanted to help, and that I could come to you with any needs I might have."

His eyes lit up. He swallowed. "Yes. I did."

"Well, actually—" She rolled her glass in a gentle circle, tranced by the golden liquid. Mustering enough courage, she took another taste. The Scotch slid down her throat, warm and comforting. "Actually, I have two requests."

Major Billet wiped his lips with his napkin. "Don't be shy, Janet. I told you we're here to help each other."

Again, she steadied her eyes on the glass, while contemplating those words. She didn't remember the 'help each other' in their conversation. But nitpicking with him would only hinder her purpose.

"I need another leave."

He cut his cabbage and sprinkled salt and pepper onto his plate. Piercing a tender piece of lamb with his fork, he held the steaming morsel up for her to see. "Lamb for officers. Did you know that?"

Janet shook her head, suddenly her mouth began to salivate over the aroma of meat, even if it were a form of mutton, which she had never been fond of.

"Did you get lamb tonight?"

"No, sir, I didn't."

He scowled. "You should have. What did you eat?"

"Tuna noodle casserole."

"You're cooking again? Did Frost come for dinner?"

Janet grimaced. "No. Major Billet, he did not. And I told you, there is nothing going on between Frost and I."

Major Billet bit into his piece of lamb and chewed, all the while glaring at her. "Time will tell," he continued, his demeanor unsettled. "I told you I would get you another leave. Yours was cut short. It's only fair. You didn't have to ask."

"Not for myself."

"Oh?"

"Lieutenant Dobi's husband is wounded and is in a hospital in Horsham. She's extremely worried about him as he hasn't written for a while. Her name is not on the list to be given a leave any time soon."

"So, you want me to break the rules?"

Janet cringed inside. Hadn't he been breaking rules all along? Hadn't he offered to break more rules for her? "My concern is for my nurses, Major. Lieutenant Dobi is not functioning at her best, and whereas her failings are not noteworthy, there is a good chance they could escalate. Giving her a few days away from here so she can visit her husband would do no harm to the ward, and would, in fact allow her peace of mind. I'm certain she would come back refreshed and willing to work harder."

The major set his fork down and sat back in his chair, his arms folded. "A lot of us haven't seen our families for months, and yet we're required to serve without complaint. Frost hasn't seen his wife for almost two years."

"He should be allowed to go home."

"That's for the Army to decide."

Janet gasped, appalled at the way the major delivered his judgment.

"What if I do grant this Lieutenant Dobi leave? What are you going to do for me?"

Janet's lips tightened. "I'll think better of you."

He raised his eyebrows and let out a laugh.

She shrugged. His games were unethical, and he could get in trouble for them. She made certain to convey that in the look she gave.

His grin disappeared, and he wiped his mouth with a napkin. "All right. I guess I'm overstepping bounds here. I'll put in a request for a three day leave for your lieutenant."

Janet guzzled the last of her scotch and stood. "Thank you, sir."

"I suppose I'm giving you quite a collection of secrets to keep in your treasure chest."

"For all the regulations you're breaking? Yes, I suppose." Janet agreed. "The treasure chest is indeed getting full. Sir."

He stood and stepped around his desk. His hand reached out to touch hers, but she stepped back. "I can't help how I feel about you, Janet."

"You'll have to, sir, if you want me to keep your secrets. Oh, and there was one other thing—"

He rolled his eyes. "I'm at your mercy."

She picked up the bottle of Johnnie Walker. He didn't say anything and neither did she. She saluted, pivoted about, and walked out the door.

 Chapter 12

Gift of a Moment

Janet jogged to hut 105, the bottle of whiskey tucked under her cape. Once inside, she wrapped it in a linen rag and stashed it in a cooler next to the cases of penicillin. So focused was she on tucking the whiskey away she didn't notice anyone else in the ward.

"Janet." Lieutenant Frost waved for her to join him. "This is First Lieutenant Richard Samson. He's just arrived from the Chinese, Burma, India Theater."

"My pleasure, Lieutenant." Janet saluted and strolled casually over to them.

"Likewise, and my pleasure to finally be in the European Theater with you good folks. You can't even imagine what this means! And just call me Sammy." The jovial man reached out to shake her hand. Short and pink cheeked, his hair thinning, his smile catching.

"All right, Sammy. I'm Janet."

"Janet!" He raised a finger. "Where have I heard that name before? Ah, yes, Scotland."

"Oh, I'm afraid we didn't meet before. I left Scotland some time ago," Janet said, hoping Sammy wasn't another ghost from the past like Major Billet had been.

"Oh no, not you." He slapped Frost's shoulder and gave out a hearty laugh. "Another Janet. A Scottish lass. I fell in love with her. There were a few Scottish gals I fell in love with. You really need to come there with me sometime, Frost. I'll hook you up."

The lieutenant shook his head, laughing. His face had turned beet red. "I don't need to hook up."

"I insist. I'll take you there soon. Before summer is over. You too, miss. What did you say your name was?"

"Lieutenant Janet Castner," she said, chuckling.

"I was introducing Sammy to our patients and going over the procedures we performed and the rehabilitation we have planned for them."

"I see! Will you be working in this ward, sir?" Janet asked.

"If I'm needed. My specialty is traumatic head injuries. So, you might see me sometimes. I like to get a sense of who is who and where before the onslaught."

"I think we've already had the onslaught."

"Yes, well you never know when there will be another."

"We were just finishing up here, Janet. Sammy and I are headed to the mess hall." He looked at his watch. "Have you eaten? Day shift doesn't get off for another half hour?"

"Thanks, Lieutenant, but I've had dinner. I wanted to check on Morrissey and see how his leg is. I don't mind starting early."

"Ah, Morrissey." Frost eyed the patient and lowered his voice. "The wound is drying up quickly and is causing him a lot of discomfort. Itching. See what you can do. If you'll excuse us," Frost bade them good evening.

"Nice to have met you, sir." Janet saluted Sammy. The two walked out the door.

The day shift nurses, Beatrice and Jean, were putting equipment away across the hall. Janet greeted them when they looked her way. "How has it been today?"

"Things have settled down," Beatrice said. "The patients are just finishing up their meal and then we're off duty. We didn't leave much for you to do. Privates Roger Stanmore, Jim Offend, and Richard Parkinson are moving into hut 108 for recovery this evening. They're all packed and ready to go. Lieutenant Frost is coming back for them after he has dinner. Keep an eye on Sergeant Rutherford, as he may need another shot of morphine before too long. His wound's been weeping. Oh, and Sergeant Morrissey's been complaining, but I don't think there's much we can do for him at this point. Everyone else is fine. Patterson is getting surgery, so he's in 110 for a while, thank heavens. I don't think I could deal with him one more day!"

"He's a handful. Thanks Bea. I'll take it from here."

The three soldiers waiting for their transfer sat at a table near the door. A deck of cards dealt out, they each smoked a cigarette and had a cup of coffee in their hands. A cane was propped up against the table. "I'm glad to see you're on the mend," Janet greeted them after the day shift nurses left.

"Almost."

"We sure do thank you for your services, ma'am." Private Stanmore rose and saluted energetically, his left hand wrapped neatly in a sling.

"You're indeed welcome, Private."

After filling a Syrette, she walked over to Sergeant Rutherford's bed. He sat upright in bed, his dinner on a tray next to him. Not a bite had been touched. "You're not hungry?"

"I'm in too much pain, nurse," he mumbled. "Makes my stomach upset."

"And yet food is what nourishes your body, makes you strong."

"Not that food."

She peeked under the tray lid. No lamb there, but a helping of cabbage and over cooked potatoes. "I see what you mean. Well, I can give you another shot to kill the pain so that you sleep tonight, but tomorrow we may have to cut down on the meds. Especially if you haven't been eating. Maybe I can bring you a tastier dinner, tomorrow." Janet dabbed his arm with alcohol and administered the drug.

His eyes closed, and he sighed. "Thanks, Lieutenant," he whispered.

"How about me? Did you bring me something tasty?" Sergeant Morrissey scooted his back against his pillow. Squinting, he cried out and despite his hand bound in a bandage, he held his leg. "Ouch! I don't know what's worse. The pain or the itch."

"I see your wrists are healing nicely."

"One is."

The wrap on his left hand had been removed, but his right hand was still bound tightly. Janet quickly pulled his blanket back. Indeed, the skin on his leg had dried and wrinkled around the open wound. "Don't move." Janet hurried to the cooler to retrieve a bottle of peanut oil. Eyeing the whiskey propped up next to the oil, she grabbed that too, along with a tin cup. Placing both bottles and cup at her feet by Morrissey's bed, she sat beside him and lifted his leg onto her lap. She poured oil generously over the dried flesh, massaging his skin until the emollient was absorbed. He winced and jerked away when her hands came near the wound.

She stopped. "Painful?"

"Excruciating!"

"All right, then." Janet poured a generous amount of scotch in the cup and handed it to him.

His eyes grew wide. "I love you."

She laughed. "You say that now."

"No, it's true." He drank greedily, downing more than half of what she had poured.

"Easy there."

He sighed, leaned back against his pillow, and closed his eyes.

Janet continue the massage until Lou's skin had absorbed the oil. When she was finished, she put a clean towel around his leg and slowly moved away. He didn't budge. The cup tipped precariously, threatening to spill, so she carefully took it away from him.

He opened his eyes. "You can't imagine what a woman's gentleness does for a man who was brought out of the field on a stretcher."

She didn't answer. He was right. Even though she'd seen films, documentaries, read books, heard testimonies from the soldiers she cared for, she had no way of knowing what it was like to be carried away, transported on a boat or plane, or truck, bleeding, hurting, traumatized. She would probably never know. She listened, because that's all she could do for him.

"You get to thinking death is the only way out. There's no softness, no kindness. People want you killed and your job is to stop them, and kill them in the process. The whole world is a bomb detonating, and you dodge the broken fragments. Ducking and rolling out of the way. Staying awake all night for fear of someone slitting your throat, or rattling you with bullets, or worse, blowing up your best buddy." He looked at her. Their eyes connected. "And then those of us lucky enough end up someplace like this. Waking up to a pretty face. Gentleness. Someone telling us things are going to be all right. That we'll live. Go home maybe." Tears welled in the corner of his eyes. "That maybe we won't die young after all. You can't imagine what that does for a soul."

She put the cup back in his hand and poured another shot worth. That got his attention, but instead of drinking it he lifted it up to her.

"Take it," he said. "I've had enough."

"Very well."

She stood and gathered her things, the peanut oil, the whiskey bottle, the cup. His eyes were open, but he lay rigid on the bed, staring off into space.

"I'll take that drink off your hands," one of the other patients offered.

Soon, other soldiers propped themselves up in their beds. Their requests became a chorus, asking for a drink, and so Janet pulled enough cups from the closet and poured a shot of whiskey for all the patients who were awake.

 Chapter 13

The Pit of War

Lou knew what she was doing, walking from bed to bed, pouring a drink for all the soldiers. Befriending them. In a sense, he was glad his fellow infantrymen were being catered to. They deserved more than a little shot of whiskey, but they'd never get what they deserved. Men who gave their bodies to stop the Nazi advance could never be honored enough. These men had seen too much. Trudged through rain with nowhere to sleep. Mud up to the knees. Slosh fused with blood that adhered to their boots, their pants, their legs, as if death had a claim on them. As if they were buried already and the grave clung to them. No medals, honors, news articles, handshakes, pats on the back, could give them the tribute they deserved. Not these guys. These fellas who lay in cots bandaged up like mummies. Some of them smiling and playing cards. Relaxed, as if nothing happened and their wounds were little more than an encumbrance. The nurse didn't know what was underneath all that gauze. She didn't know the real wounds that all these soldiers bore. She'd never know.

Lou shut his eyes tight. He tried to relive that day before they reached St. Lo. If only someone could have gone into town to warn the residents. If only those mamas had word, they could have gone to a shelter. Time doesn't bend for anyone, though, so he just lay there with his eyes shut, playing the scene over and over in his mind.

"Hey." Someone shook his shoulder. "Lou, come out of it."

Lou opened his eyes. A man leaned over him and offered Lou his cup. "C'mon. Drink. I saved you some."

"Ray! What are you doing here? You're supposed to be in France." Lou's voice cracked, he was so surprised to see his friend.

"Yeah, so are you."

"I'll be there. Give me a minute." He joked, cracking a half smile which vanished when a spasm of pain darted through his leg.

"War's over for you, it looks like." Ray sat on Lou's bed.

"It's just a scratch."

"I can tell."

Lou grunted in disagreement, but he knew Ray was right. He wouldn't be going back to the front for some time, if ever. "Did you see Paris?" he asked his friend.

"For a split second. Got hit riding into town. How about you?"

If Lou had seen victory in Paris, the memory had been erased. "I didn't get that far. All I saw was an explosion on the way there, and then this. So many dead."

"War's hell," Ray added.

"Makes you wonder if it's worth it to go on. If there's anything any of us can do to fix this godforsaken world."

Ray looked him in the eye. "We owe it to the world to try and fix it. Sure, we're getting shot up. All of us soldiers are. But someone has to defend the innocent."

"I've seen a lot of innocents die right there in France," Lou whispered. "Our gunners were the ones that killed them."

"I know." Ray sighed heavily and looked away. "There's no excuse. But the truth is, if our forces weren't coming against Hitler, the damage would be worse."

"I believe that."

"If you keep thinking about the loss, the life in you will vaporize. Like that candle there." He nodded toward the flame that flickered on the table by Lou's bed. Ray pinched open the dam of melting liquid that all but smothered the wick. The wax trickled down the side of the candle and the flame burned brighter. "Don't lose your light, Lou," he said, softly.

"I'll get over it," Lou assured him.

"Better sooner than later. I saw you with that nurse. She takes kindly to you. We can all see it. You've been around the bad guys too long. It's messed up your head. That was a special kind of compassion she showed you just now. She's partial to you. You know what I'm saying?"

"I think so."

"Let it come. Embrace it. You're letting all this war stuff get to your head."

Maybe Ray was right. He gave another friendly pat on Lou's shoulder and nodded, holding the cup of whiskey for him to take. "Don't be looking a gift horse in the mouth. She's a cutie. You're crazy not to let her help you."

Lou hadn't noticed the room before, but several patients looked their way.

"Don't disillusion him, Ray," one of them said. "The doctor and that nurse are like this." He held up his crossed fingers and everyone laughed. "Heard they're going to the officers' dance next weekend."

"That's right. Glen Miller. If that isn't a hot date, I don't know what is."

The teasing went on, and the subject rolled so far off course that they were no longer talking about nurses and doctors, but about baseball, and horse races, and pubs, and wives back home. Lou thought of his mother and father, and their house in Cincinnati and the job he left behind. He thought about Jack and the day they swore an oath to fight for the good old USA. He wondered where Jack was. Ray's eyes were pinned to him, as if the man could read his thoughts.

"Some of us die for our country in battle, that's one honorable thing. But we don't die because we give up." He shook his head. "That doesn't help anyone. You know what I mean? It doesn't make your friends happy either."

"Okay Ray," Lou said quietly so the others couldn't hear. "Okay."

 Chapter 14

The Officer's Dance

Janet studied herself in the mirror. "I swear someday I'll be able to change my clothes again."

"When I get home, I'm going to buy everything yellow. Dresses, scarves, hats. Shoes too," Sue said, spitting on her fingers and winding a lock of hair into a curl. "I'm getting me one of those fancy curling irons, too."

"Blue for me, but not navy blue. Blue like the sky." Marty tightened her belt.

"Like the sky? That would be gray," Sue corrected.

"I mean the sky in California. I'm getting heels too."

They wore dull army-green dresses, buttoned down the front, flared skirt, pockets. Uniforms. Apparel meant only for special occasions but still uniforms.

"I'm so tired of this color." Janet moved away from the mirror.

"I almost forgot!" Sue jumped up, snapping her fingers. "We're going to be styling tonight." Sue shuffled through boxes under her bed and pulled out a small paper bag. "You won't believe what I bought at that little five and dime."

"Cigarette holders! Red!" Marty clapped her hands.

"Same color as our fingernail polish." Sue held up her freshly polished fingernails. Tossing her hair and letting the waves fall over one eye, she held the holder to her lips and struck a pose.

"If I didn't know you better, I'd mistake you for Lauren Bacall." Janet laughed. "Give me one of those."

"We're going to be a hit tonight, ladies," Marty announced.

"Especially Janet, since she gets Errol Flynn Frost as an escort."

Janet laughed. No matter how many times she told them Frost was married, they still teased her.

Lieutenant Frost met Janet at the crossroads, while Sue and Marty walked ahead of them. Clouds loomed overhead, but no rain fell. She hooked her arm into his as they strolled along the darkening trail, partly to use him as a support to keep from turning her ankle, and partly because she liked the security of being next to him.

"How are things in 105?" he asked. "I didn't have a chance to go back after I moved the transfers."

"For the most part, things are stable. Whose doing Patterson's surgery?"

"McCall."

"I hope it changes his attitude. The nurses are glad for the break."

"I bet they are."

"I worry about Rutherford. He begs for morphine and I think we need to cut his dosage. I also worry about Morrissey."

"Why Morrissey?"

"Depression. CSR. He's a troubled man. The Allied bombing of St. Lo did a number on him. I wish I could help."

"So that's it." Frost grew quiet, a look of contemplation crossed his face. His attention fell away from her. He watched the ground as they walked, and she, curious yet respectful of his space, took in the festive lights which beckoned them into Petworth.

The rumor had been that the famous Glen Miller's band would be making an appearance. From the sound of the saxophones echoing against the apartment buildings, the gossip was correct. The entire town came alive as more than just army officers filled the street. Soldiers lingered outside, smoking, socializing, their dates laughing, flirting. Feet tapping to the easy brass tempo. Janet hadn't seen so many smiles for a long time.

Janet hadn't noticed anything unusual about the crowd until they approached a circle of partiers. Two soldiers were in their midst, loaded with liquor, talking loudly enough for her to hear.

"Starving, that's what they are over there. Starving and lost in the jungle! Our own soldiers!" Drool formed at the corner of the young soldier's lips.

"Leeches, malaria, snakes. Every kind of disease you can imagine. Corpses bloating, and you can't bury them because there ain't no dirt. Foot rot. Everyone has foot rot. You don't get rid of it either. The whole jungle stinks like death and that's fifteen miles from the front. You pack in and if you get hit, someone packs you out. If you're lucky you both aren't ambushed on the way back. No telling what happens to our POWs. Heard they execute their prisoners. Slow death. Nurses too. The place is a hellhole. Grass shacks for a hospital with no walls. No way of getting out of the rain. Once you're there, they don't transfer you either, unless you're dying," the other added.

"Then how'd you get here?" someone from the crowd asked.

The soldier spat on the ground and pulled open his shirt, revealing a scar that looked as though he'd been pierced by a bamboo rod. "It ain't healed neither," he said. "Might be the death of me. They sent most everyone down under but Jed and me. We're the only wounded guys that didn't get malaria, so they sent us here. Better say your prayers you don't go to Burma."

"Come on," Frost ushered Janet into the hall. "I don't need to listen to that."

"Their talk kind of validates the rumors I heard about CBI," Janet said.

"Me too." He led her to the refreshment table. "But there's always the chance of being transferred there."

Janet knew many of the people in the hall. Staff from 104th General Hospital swarmed the place, and not only medical personnel but British officers from surrounding cities who had come with their wives.

Janet nibbled at the refreshments and engaged in small talk with the other nurses. She laughed when she eyed Marty across the hall pull out her bright red cigarette holder. The band played the first notes of "Moonlight Serenade", Lieutenant Frost took her hand, and led her to the dance floor.

"Nice," he whispered, leading her in a fox trot.

Assuming he meant the evening, the music, the relief from everything having to do with war, Janet couldn't agree more. "I'll say."

"Sometimes getting away is just what the doctor ordered."

"No pun intended," Janet laughed. Surprised at his solemn expression, she gave him an inquisitive glance.

"Our patients could use something like this. I feel guilty being here while the boys who have been doing the dirty work are back in the ward suffering. A little TLC would bring them out of depression."

"They're hardly capable of dancing."

He shrugged, still serious. "We'll have to wean Rutherford off morphine. I think it's possible. His wounds are slow healing what with that shattered femur bone. But there are less addictive drugs we can use to ease the pain."

"And Morrissey?"

"He's withdrawing, mild case of battle fatigue. The only thing you and I can do to help is to be kind."

"That shouldn't be too hard."

When the music ended, Frost hooked her arm in his and guided her to a quiet corner. "McCall is anxious to move Morrissey out of the ward."

"Why?"

"He can't stand to see an idle body. You know how he is. Stick to the books. Sew them up and move them out. I'd like to keep Morrissey for a few weeks more until we're certain his leg is healed."

"How can we do that if McCall has other plans?"

"I'm not sure. We might be able to convince McCall that Morrissey would heal faster if he has a better outlook on life."

"How would we do that?"

"Get his attention off his leg. Get him out of bed, out of the ward if you can. Bring him into town. His wrists are healing fine. He has use of both his hands. And he can start walking. I'll put a brace on his leg in the morning, so he'll be capable of mild activity with crutches. I don't see why he wouldn't be able to sit through a movie."

Before she could respond, the stiff angry glare of Major Billet caught her eye. He moved through the crowd directly toward them.

"Oh, good lord, brace yourself," she whispered as she stepped back away from Frost.

"Lieutenants!" Major Billet's voice chimed like a brass symbol.

Frost turned to face him and saluted.

"Fancy seeing you two together here," the major said, a snide twist to his tongue.

"Lieutenant Castner needed an escort tonight, Major, sir." Frost stood tall. Daring.

"Yes, I can tell. I'll take it from here, Lieutenant. You're dismissed."

Janet's eyes widened. She stuttered to defend Frost, but he dodged away before she could speak—and before she could refuse Major Billet the dance that had just begun. Another foxtrot. Their hands clasped, he slid the other to the small of her back. Suddenly a queasy sensation passed through her stomach.

"So," he began. "You and Frost have no relationship?"

"We have a purely professional relationship. We were actually discussing the patients."

"I see," he said. The smirk on his face one of unbelief. "Not that it matters."

"No, not that it matters," she agreed, matching his sneer.

"Except he could very easily find himself transferred to Burma."

"That would be highly unfair."

"You think?" He swung her around in beat to the music. The spin startled her. She bit her lip when she returned, more angry than surprised. "I have authority to instate a transfer if I so choose. As discipline."

"What discipline? What has he done? Walked me here from the hospital and asked for one lousy dance?"

"Yes."

"And you dancing with me isn't fraternizing?"

"Not when I'm commander of this post, no." The music ended. He released his hold on her and bowed slightly. "Be forewarned. Lieutenant Frost is a good doctor. I would hate to send him to the brush of Burma, but I will if I need to." With that, he clicked his heels, pivoted about and walked away.

Janet waited until she could no longer see him, slid out of the hall, and jogged down the street. Once in the shadows, she let the tears flow. Avoiding Frost would be difficult, but not as difficult as seeing him transferred to a rabid jungle.

 Chapter 15

Solace

Having left the streets of Petworth alone and upset, Janet jogged along the muddy trail in the dark of night. With only the glint of starlight reflected on a distant Nissen hut, she found her way through the lonely stretch of fields to the hospital. Chilled and out of breath, her nerves settled as she approached ward 105. With the night still young, and Janet too upset to go home, she decided to check on her patients, secretly hoping that Morrissey was still awake.

She opened the door, startling the young intern inside. The nurse stood at attention and saluted.

"At ease, Lieutenant," Janet returned her salute. "Anything exciting happening in here?" She held the back of a chair to immobilize her trembling hands.

"No, ma'am. I was sorting through these supplies that came today. Are you okay?"

"Yes, I'm fine. How are the patients?" Janet scoped out the room. Most of the men were asleep, but Ray Richardson and Vern Jennings sat up in their beds, reading. Morrissey had a parchment in his hands, but his eyes were fixed on her. Her heart skipped a beat. "I'll take care of things now," Janet told the nurse. "Take the rest of the evening off."

"But, I thought you were … I mean the dance?"

"I was. You're dismissed." Janet gave the girl a cordial nod. Ray had been watching Janet. When she looked at him, he glanced at Morrissey, shut his book and rolled over in his bed. Vern also tucked his journal away and slipped under his covers. Morrissey made no movement whatsoever.

She turned off the overhead light, struck a match and lit a lantern, illuminating the room just enough to find her way around the cots, but not enough to disturb the sleeping soldiers. She moved quietly among them, feeling their foreheads, pulling the blankets up over their shoulders, and tucking them all in for the night. When she got to Morrissey's bed, she paused, her eyes locked on his.

"What's wrong?" he whispered.

"Wrong? You're doing much better. I see your wrists are healing quickly. They took the wraps off!"

"Not me. You."

Janet eyed the patients on the beds next to Lou's cot, embarrassed and hoping no one heard. "Nothing," she started.

"Have a seat." He patted the bed. Janet paused, not certain if she should accept his invitation. Having recovered from the jaunt from Petworth, why did her heart still thunder? There was no reason to be hot, but when she looked into his eyes, she felt feverish. She sat down.

"Something wrong?"

"No. I must have walked too quickly, is all. I'm a little faint but I'll be all right." Remembering Lieutenant's Frost's request, she thought perhaps this would be the perfect time to help Morrissey out of his slump.

He scooted over to make more room for her. His eyes were wide open and alert.

"You appear stronger," she said.

"I have a wonderful nurse."

She laughed. "I don't know about wonderful."

"I do. Look, I wanted to apologize," he said.

"Whatever for?"

"For sulking like a little kid. For turning my back on you. I should have been more gracious."

Completely taken aback, she patted his hand. "You don't have to apologize—"

"No. But I do."

"Okay then, your apology is accepted."

His stare made her nervous. She shuffled uncomfortably, about to rise but he clasped her hand. His touch calmed her. He leaned forward and stroked her cheek gently with his thumb. She didn't balk or move away. Her flesh tingled under his fingertips, and a warm sensation filled her body.

"You've been crying." His voice was barely audible, and he frowned. "What's wrong?"

"Don't be silly. Everything's fine." She spoke as softly as he did.

"You came back from the officer's dance before it was over. That's not normal. Something happened. What?"

"Oh—well—" she stuttered.

"You should be there, away from all of us war-torn soldiers."

"Too much noise," she lied.

"Did you have a falling out with your date?"

She gaped at him and lost control of her voice. "I wasn't on a date, Sergeant." She spoke so loudly that her voice cracked. They both looked around the room.

A chuckle came from one of the beds behind her and she turned around to catch the heckler. She couldn't tell which man laughed. All she saw were bodies covered up and heads buried under pillows.

"Word travels fast in places like this," Lou warned, raising a finger to her lips and whispering.

"Well, whatever word is traveling, it's the wrong word!"

He shook his head, his expression solemn. "You and the doctor aren't an item?"

"No. Lieutenant Frost is married. He's faithful to his wife and there is absolutely nothing between us. Though I have no idea why I'm telling you."

"Whoa! Easy, sweetheart!" Lou laughed. "No need to get upset."

There were lots of reasons to be upset, but they weren't his bother. She held back tears, though it was a fight. "You're right. No reason to get upset. Not at you, anyway." She forced a smile and studied his face. The drugs must have worn off because the sergeant had a healthy twinkle in his eyes. "How are you feeling?"

"Better. My leg still hurts but I can bear the pain now."

"Lieutenant Frost is going to put a splint on your leg tomorrow, so you can get out and move around a bit."

"I went outside today."

"You did?"

"I needed a cigarette, some fresh air. Your intern helped me get to the door and I leaned up against it outside. I could hear the music all the way from town. Bothers me that you left. You should be there having a good time."

"I wasn't having all that much fun."

"Why not?"

What could she say to him without incriminating Major Billet? Rumor would get around quickly enough, and if that happened, the major would take the steps necessary to quiet her. He would probably transfer her out of the unit. Where else would she be sent, but to Burma?

Lou swung his legs over the side of the bed. "Come to think of it, there are a million stars out. I need another smoke, what about you?"

Janet steadied him as he leaned on her and with the blanket over his shoulders, she helped him hobble to the door and step into the clear night air. Lou propped himself against the wall, pulled a pack of smokes from his pocket, and offered her a cigarette.

"Thanks," she said.

Though the hills were dark, and only a few lights in the distance marked Petworth, stars glimmered like jewels above their heads. Music from the dance she had left echoed through the valley, and for a few moments, the disappointment of not being there bothered her. Marty and Sue were probably having a great time, flirting with the single officers, drinking cocktails, nibbling on fancy hors d'oeuvres and dancing the fox trot. Lieutenant Frost was probably worrying about what had happened to her.

Major Billet was probably smirking to himself, puffed up like a rooster, prideful of the power he exercised over her. That alone would be reason to go back. However, if she did return she'd be putting Frost in peril. No. Leaving was the better choice. Let the major win his battle. There would be other dances.

"I don't know what happened," Lou interrupted her thoughts. He puffed on his cigarette, and when she looked at him he went on, "... but if I were at that dance, I would have made certain you had a good time."

"Thanks," Janet whispered. "That's kind of you."

"If I could, I would dance with you even now."

She let his words sink in before she spoke because they gave her strength. Confidence. "Thank you, but that's not exactly what happened. I wasn't hurting for someone to dance with. There were actually too many people that wanted my attention." She peered at him, hoping she hadn't said too much. He scowled but didn't dig for any more information.

"I can understand that." He flicked the burnt embers from the tip of his cigarette. "A pretty gal like you. You must be very popular among the officers."

She shrugged, leaned against the hut and listened to the sound of the sax echo through the valley. Not until he spoke again did she realize he'd been staring at her.

"The music sounds better from here," he added.

She laughed. "Does it? Why's that?"

"Because I get to listen to it with you by my side."

"Silly." She brushed off his flattery, but she couldn't brush off his genuineness. His remarkable green eyes sparkled in the starlight. "But I'm glad you feel that way," she said.

"You are? Why?"

"Because now you won't mind me asking you to go to town with me as soon as you can walk."

"Really?"

"Lieutenant Frost suggested you get away from here for the day. He thinks you're too depressed."

"Don't I get the prize?" Lou laughed. "Now I'm convinced you two aren't hooked. What man would donate a day with a pretty nurse like yourself to a crippled infantry fella?"

"All in the line of duty, soldier," she said. "Keep that in mind."

"Of course."

 Chapter 16

All about CBI

"Thirteen nurses got transferred today." Sue raced into the hut, waking Janet from a deep sleep by pinching her toes.

"Hey!" Janet sat up.

Sue paced animatedly across the room.

"Did you see the list?" Marty asked. "Oh God, I hope it isn't me."

"No, not to worry. I looked for both your names. You're safe. The list is posted in the mess hall."

"Who? Anyone you know?"

"Dolores. They're sending her to CBI. She's devastated. I'm going over to her hut to see if I can be of comfort. Everyone on the list is going to CBI."

Janet gasped, remembering Major Billet's threat the night before. "Are you sure I'm not on the list? What about Lieutenant Frost? Did you see if Frost is on the list?"

Sue had already left.

"What's with sending everyone to Burma? My sister might be enlisting. Do you think she'll have to go?" Janet asked.

"I don't know, Janet, but you might want to write and tell her. I have a cousin talking about joining the Corps too. I'm going to check the list. Be right back." Marty grabbed her coat and raced out the door. Janet jumped out of bed, but before she could get fully dressed, Lieutenant Dobi peeked inside.

"Lieutenant Castner, I just wanted to drop by and say thank you. I've been waiting a couple of months, and I finally got my leave."

"Come in, Lieutenant." Janet stood and returned the woman's salute. Dressed in a green summer dress with a v-line collar, and her hair tied back in a bun, Dobi had a suitcase in each of her white gloved hands. Janet felt a tad envious, not only that Dobi got to leave for a few days to see her husband, but also that she was dressed in civilian clothes. "Congratulations. How long a leave did they give you?"

Dobi cleared her throat and kept her head bowed when she answered. "Three days, ma'am."

Janet laughed in wonderment. "Two suitcases and a bag?"

Dobi shrugged and refused to look her in the eye. "I just wanted to say thank you. I can't wait to see Joey. Everything is all set. There's a taxi waiting for me that's going take me right to where he's at. Thank you." She peered up at her again. "I appreciate what you've done."

"My pleasure, Lieutenant. Have a good trip. See you in a couple of days."

Dobi didn't answer. She grabbed her bags and hurried out the door just as Marty returned.

"Sue's right, we're not listed. And the men's list isn't up yet but there's rumor it's a long one. What's up with Dobi?" Marty asked.

"She got her leave."

"What did she say to you?" Marty glance down the road and scowled as the young nurse walked hurriedly toward a waiting cab.

"She thanked me. Why do you ask?"

"She acted kind of strange when I passed her on my way to the mess hall. Mumbled to herself something fierce."

"What did she say?"

"'Thank you, God', repeatedly. She looked at me and said she's glad she's leaving."

"Of course, she is. She's going to see her husband. What did you think she meant?"

"I don't know. The way she said her prayers, you'd think she was getting out of the Army for good." Marty moved inside the hut, and Janet followed.

"Well, I wouldn't worry too much about Dobi. Everyone wants to see their spouses. She's one lucky gal, getting to spend a couple of days with her honey. Imagine being in Dobi's shoes–running off to see your sweetheart. It must be nice. Wish I had a honey to visit." Janet shut the door.

"Don't we all!" Marty slung her uniform jacket over her shoulder. "What's wrong with us?"

"I think we spend too much time reading romance novels," Janet replied.

"Speaking of romance novels, my cousin just sent me a best seller. *Forever Amber* by Kathleen Winsor."

"What's it about?"

"A 17th century lady who works her way up through British society by having lovers."

"Whoa, For shame! Let me see!" Janet inspected the cover. "Dibs when you're done." She handed the book back to Marty. "Right now, I'm worried about Frost. I hope he isn't getting transferred. I'd die if we had to work with McCall every day. The man's a monster." Janet reached for her coat.

"Wait! Aren't you cooking breakfast? All they have over there is grits and egg mix." Marty pleaded.

"Not this morning. I need to get moving." Janet buttoned her coat.

"Where are you going?"

"I'm taking a soldier to town."

"No way!" Marty exclaimed. "How did that happen?"

"It was Frost's suggestion. He said Morrissey needs to get out of the ward and see some sunlight."

"There isn't any."

"Well then, he needs to see some clouds, I guess."

"Morrissey is it?"

Janet smiled, remembering the night before–how kind his words were toward her, how beautiful the stars shone in the crisp night air. How warm his presence made her just standing next to him.

"Nothing's going on, is it?" Marty hinted.

Janet shrugged. "I've got to go."

"But breakfast?"

"Come on, Marty, make some oatmeal if you don't like grits."

Marty's bed bounced when she fell on it. "What's the difference?"

Janet laughed and placed her hat on her head. "Toughen up, soldier."

"Right."

The sun had risen, but only a dim light illuminated the camp, and a cool mist wet her face as she stepped outside. Folks were beginning to make their way from the mess hall. Two nurses raced past her, angst on their faces. Janet's heart grew heavy.

"Castner!" a man's voice called out, stopping her in her tracks. The lieutenant that Frost had introduced to her, the one who had arrived from CBI jogged up to her.

"Good morning Lieutenant," Janet greeted him. "Sammy, correct? How's the world treating you this morning?"

"Better than some, I must say." He eyed the nurses Janet had been watching. "Pity. Burma's no place for the ladies. Nurse or not."

"Tell me more!"

They walked slowly, and Lieutenant Samson shook his head as he recalled his experiences. "Hot, humid, and bug infested. Rain never did cool us off. Soaked us to the core so that our whole bodies turned white and wrinkled up, like what happens when you're in the tub too long. Supplies were a luxury. I don't know how often we had to do our own foraging for food."

"You foraged for food?"

He chuckled. "We did. Threw hand grenades in the river. Fish floated belly up and then we grabbed them."

"Brutal!"

"We saw more death there than any hospital I've ever been in. The hospitals are grass shacks, poorly protected from mosquitos. The Chinese patients wouldn't cooperate one iota. They refused to take orders from women, so I was the emissary, speaking on the ladies' behalf just to keep the sick ones in bed."

Janet held back a laugh.

Sammy frowned. "These were patients that were supposed to be isolated, but they spread disease instead. Malaria. Too many men died from malaria. Too many."

"That's horrible," Janet said.

"Not to mention infestation of mites. And dysentery. Worse, the Japs are ruthless. They've imprisoned nurses, as well as soldiers. Don't know how many are POWs right now. Too many. Glad you don't have to go, Lieutenant. Where are you headed now?"

"I'm getting one of our patients out and about this morning. Look. That must be my taxi." She nodded at the black motor coach idling at the end of the alley. The driver acknowledged her wave. "Why do you ask?"

"Next week I'm meeting with a couple of pilots and we're flying to Scotland for the day. Think you and your friends might want to join us?"

"That's tempting. I'll see what my friends say."

"Good. We'd love your company."

He saluted, and with a hop, turned back the way he had come, leaving Janet to ponder over what he had told her about Burma—convinced now, more than ever, that she was indeed fortunate to be in the European Theater.

When Janet opened the door to 105 to get Lou, she nearly bumped into Lieutenant Frost. Major McCall was in the room with him, packing medical bags. She met his eyes—a cold, cruel stare.

"Sir!" she saluted McCall. "Good morning, Lieutenant," she said to Frost. He looked away from her.

What kind of reception was that—unless an enterprise put into play by Major Billet. With the impending threat hanging over Frost, had McCall been asked to keep an eye on him?

She shut the door and swept past the two, into the hut and toward Morrissey's bed. The soldier, dressed for a trip to town, sat upright, his wounded leg in a cast. Crutches leaned against the bedpost next to him.

Damp air chilled the room when McCall and Frost walked out the door. Neither said goodbye, but the Lieutenant gave her a remorseful glance. Anger brewed, and Janet opened her mouth to vent. Fortunately, Morrissey interrupted her thoughts.

"I'm ready, ma'am." He grinned. "Looking forward to this!"

"I am too." Making a conscious effort to forget the injustice that polluted the camp, she pulled the soldier's coat from the wall, helped him into it, and handed him his crutches. When he leaned on her to steady himself, the closeness felt strangely comforting, and yet forbidden. She inched away from him. "The taxi's out there now. Can you manage?" she asked.

"I'm a little lopsided, but I'll be fine." A seriousness came over him. "How about you?"

Curious as to whether he overheard any relevant conversations before she arrived, she stood speechless for a moment. "Me? I'm fine. Let's go."

The nurse on duty gave her a hard look. A patient who'd been staring turned away quickly when Janet acknowledged him. The odd silence suggested that she had been a topic of conversation–the muteness thick, the gazes too guilt-ridden. Janet followed the hobbling Morrissey outside. "The taxi's parked a bit far down the road," she apologized.

"Good. I'm looking forward to a nice long walk."

"The road is uneven. The walk might be hard on you."

He stopped abruptly. Leaning heavily on his crutch, he turned to look at her. "Hard on me? No. The battles in France were hard on me. Walking alongside a pretty nurse will be a breeze."

The mist seemed to evaporate as they stared at each other. The sun burned a hole in the clouds and shone on his face, making the green of his eyes even more vivid, his torment even clearer.

"My physical wounds will be fine, don't you worry." He grimaced as he held out his leg. "This isn't the pain that hurts."

Janet took a breath and waited for her insides to calm before she spoke. So many emotions spewed from him, she needn't cause any more. "Thanks for reminding me how tough you fellas are." Her sincerity swayed him, it seemed, for he gave her a wide smile and pulled a cigarette from his pocket, cuffed his hands around the tip to light it, and then blew smoke into the breeze, away from her.

"Sorry. Don't mean to be irritable with you. Lieutenant. You're just doing your job."

"And I can do my job better if I know what to work on."

Time seemed to stand still as they studied each other. Mending his heart was not her duty. She was a nurse. She enlisted to fix gunshot wounds and bleeding bodies. Nothing in the contract with the Red Cross deemed her responsible for broken hearts. Yet something about this man compelled her to find a cure for his despair. And if she weren't mistaken, it seemed to her—as he leaned on his crutches and considered her eyes—he begged for her help.

He spoke softly. "I don't think you can mend those lesions, ma'am. I don't think anyone can. They're wounds that just need to scar over."

"Well, I know a good place to start." She nodded in the direction of Petworth. The grassy field beamed with morning sunlight as the clouds drifted away, and beyond where red gables and chimneys dotted the hills in-between the trees. "Let's forget about war today." She started down the road to the idling taxi. He followed, limping awkwardly.

She waited for him at the cab.

"They say the joy is in the journey," Lou said. "If that's true, then we're going to have a grand old time."

Chapter 17

The Antique Shoppe

He enjoyed her attention, and he'd be thrilled if it were sincere. He didn't, however trust the motive as to why had she coerced him out of bed to bring him to town. If indeed this was just another medical procedure recommended by his doctor, and all in the line of duty, like she said, then how would it help anything? He'd love for her to want to spend time with him away from the hospital, away from the war, away from doctors and procedures, and regulations. But that was not what this was about. She was a nurse, and this was his therapy.

Maybe he'd be better off staying in bed.

The hospital staff wanted him to accept that because he was hurt, the war was over for him. Or because he wasn't returning to France, he should forget what happened there.

How could he forget? How could he return to normalcy? Was he supposed to forget his friends who were in the trenches, risking their lives, getting shot up, and torn apart? Was he supposed to ignore the thousands of soldiers who drew their last breath today, cramped in a bloody hole somewhere, dodging enemy bullets on foreign soil they had never seen before? Nor would ever see again?

If that was Janet's plan, it wouldn't work. He couldn't shut them out. He hadn't enlisted in the army to desert his troops. Loitering around in this quaint British town, taking in a movie—as if an escape from reality would mend his heartache—wasn't going to fix anything. He was forsaking his men and the silent oath he took to stay by their side.

He watched Janet as she walked. Her strong attractive body silhouetted against the rising sun, threads of her neatly combed hair flying in the breeze like golden angel locks. Her world so distant from his. Sure, she rolled up her sleeves and subdued his fever, washed his leg, and doused him with alcohol and peanut oil or whatever other potions she had to make him feel better. But her attempts to take him away from his buddies out in the field—if not in body, then in heart and mind—would be fruitless. He refused to leave them. He'd be with them until the day he died, even if he lived to be a hundred. Even if they sent him back to the States. Even if Hitler surrendered tomorrow.

Not until she stopped at that little antique retailer did the sun's reflection on the window brighten his thoughts. The bell rang when she opened the door. A soft, wistful ring which reminded him of his childhood when he lived on Lincoln Street.

His mom would wake him in the morning and send him to the corner grocer for milk. She always gave him an extra penny so he could stop at the sweet shop on his way home. The candy store had a bell just like this one.

"Oh, I love this place," Janet said.

Lou paused, resting his aching leg and shoulder, now sore from the crutch rubbing against his underarm. He nodded for her to go in.

"You don't mind?"

"Not at all." He followed her inside and leaned against the wall by the door. She mumbled something about antiques and moved quickly through the aisles. A childlike innocence beamed across her face, as if she hadn't seen so many beautiful items in all her life. She looked like a little girl in a doll house. His heart softened. This was no ruse. She was sincerely beautiful. Her smile innocent. The twinkle in her eye took him back to better times. Peaceful times. Summer days when he was young, when life was good.

Maybe there was something to this therapy, after all. War wasn't just about protecting his troops. Maybe his service in the Army was about protecting the good times and the good people–innocent people—like Janet. She turned and grinned at him and he knew then he wanted to live in her world. He wanted to laugh again. He wanted the same joy which shone in her eyes, and in her smile.

He walked up to her. That's when he saw the cotton apron with dainty pink flowers, laced pockets, and a yellow ribbon. He took it down from the shelf, unfolded it, and stepped behind her. Slipping the apron over her head was a bold thing to do, but the closer he got to her, the braver he became. The contact made his heart thunder–just being near to her. She laughed when he tied the bow. He kept tying it because he didn't want the moment to end. He didn't want her to stop laughing. Her voice resonated as music to his ears. He hadn't experienced that much pleasure in a long time.

The shop owner's wide eyes surprised him when she slipped around the corner. Had he done something wrong? Was the old woman going to accuse him of stealing? He quickly pulled the knots apart, pulled it up over Janet's head, made a sorry attempt at folding it, grabbed his crutches and limped hastily to the front of the store.

Janet came to his side like a mother hen returning to her nest, the apron in hand. He failed to hear the conversation, his heart beat so rapidly. The words "Nazis" and "bombed" and "children" vibrated in his ears. He made no sense out of what the old woman said. Not until the shop owner handed Janet a bag of blankets and mumbled something about how much the American G.I.s helped the British, did he let his guard down. The woman wasn't an enemy. She was a friend who had dwarfed Janet with her gifts.

"And keep the apron, dear. My mother made it. It's yours. I don't want your money."

"Can we leave this here until we're headed back?" Janet asked.

"Oh, of course. I close at five."

The woman studied him up and down after she took the bag from Janet's arms. She scrutinized Janet, pairing them as if they were lovers, or married. Lou flushed, sweat beaded on his temples. Janet opened the door for him as he gathered his crutches.

"What?" she asked.

How could he answer? His mind spun faster than a rifled bullet. Glad that she hadn't said anything on the way to the theater, he used the time to sort out the chaos. This was war, but the sun shone, the streets reminded him of home, the people went about their way as if they knew nothing of the world he'd come from. They made assumptions that—even though he wished they were—had no basis in truth.

Janet turned around and waited for him. Then reality made its horrifying entrance once again. He knew it would.

A siren—high, shrill, menacing.

Screams, shouts and the droning of a buzz-bomber.

"Take cover!" The voice was his own. It came from his gut. From fear!

Lou dove for cover, grabbing Janet as he fell, hovering over her. He heard a 'pop' and a spasm of pain darted up his leg. He winced, yet calmed Janet with a steady and gentle hold. With his other hand, he reached for his belt, for his grenade or his gun. Nothing. He was unarmed. He closed his eyes and whispered to Janet. To himself. "Easy!"

He froze. Rigid.

The bomber passed over them and faded into the distance. Janet moved, and he let her free. She reached for his crutches and helped him back up.

Graceful. A lady. He had acted rashly. Bold and insensitive. He had no right grabbing her the way he had. He flushed, embarrassed. His leg hurt more than before and when she attempted to help him to his feet, he could barely stand.

"I'm sorry," he said. "I hope I didn't hurt you."

She asked how he was. Even though his leg ached, he lied. He had no right to worry her, not after pushing her to the ground. "I'm fine," he said. "Let's go."

Despite the pain, he sat through the show, *And Now Tomorrow*. Big movie names, Susan Hayward, Loretta Young, Alan Lad. He held little interest in the story. An attractive deaf woman and her cheating fiancé who should have seen her through her illness but instead made moves for her sister. Life's too short to be unfaithful. He'd seen too many of his buddies worry about their sweethearts back home. Too many hearts were broken in real life.

"Do you want some popcorn?" Janet asked.

Food was the last thing on his mind. "No."

"Is there something wrong?"

He closed his eyes. What world should he remain faithful to? The one with bombs and cannons and dying soldiers? Or the sparkly world of sunshine he caught a glimpse of just moments before? The world named Janet.

"There's a war going on," he said, and then he wished he hadn't.

 Chapter 18

Hard Benches

Janet could tell Lou was uncomfortable by the way his whole body strained to move, so when he refused to leave early, she was surprised.

"Watch the rest of the movie. I'm fine," he whispered in her ear.

"I'm a nurse, Sergeant Morrissey. I know what pain looks like, and you are in pain."

"It's nothing."

"Shh." Someone behind them complained. Janet sat back in her seat, though she couldn't enjoy the show worrying about her patient. Had she made yet another mistake by bringing him here?

When the movie ended, she gave him a hand to help him stand. He seemed to struggle more than before. "I shouldn't have brought you here. What's wrong? Did you hurt yourself when the bomber flew over, earlier?"

Lou didn't answer, but he didn't need to. He strained to maintain his balance and winced with every move.

She helped him to the lobby. "Wait here while I flag down a cab."

"I'm coming with you."

"Sit."

"Don't tell me to sit. It's stuffy in here. I can barely breathe."

"Why are men so stubborn?" She had no choice but to bring him with her, for he refused to stay behind.

"It's how we get things done," he answered.

Much to her dismay, rain beat heavily, flooding the street. Lamppost reflections on the cobblestone glistened eerily, as if the sun had already set and they'd lost the day entirely. Janet glanced at her watch. The four o'clock hour had barely begun and not a cab in sight.

Sergeant Lou Morrissey needed to be back in the hospital and she needed to report to duty. "Don't tell me we're stranded," she whispered as she inspected life along the narrow roadway.

"Go get your blankets from the antique store," Lou urged her. "I'll wait for you here and if I see a taxi, I'll flag him."

Janet scrambled down the sidewalk and Lou waited outside the theater.

Nearly slipping on the slick pavement, she burst into the shop just as the merchant flipped the open sign in the window to closed.

"I didn't think you were coming back," the woman said.

Janet brushed the water off her cape and caught her breath while waiting for the woman to return with the bag. "You have a ride back, don't you?"

"We'll be taking a cab."

"Take care of that young man of yours." The woman patted her on the shoulder and gave her a knowing wink.

"Yes, I will," Janet answered, pushing the door open and stepping outside. Why the woman thought Sergeant Morrissey was her 'young man', she didn't know. Although the idea of being coupled with him seemed alluring–and completely against regulations.

Janet hurried back to the theater. Evening pressed on and the only vehicles visible were a lone land rover and a Humber Army vehicle parked by a flat a few blocks away. The local bus rolled through puddles, taking its load of passengers from the movie house in the opposite direction of the hospital. Lou stood alone outside the theater. She joined him, soaked now, as the hood to her cape did not keep her hair dry. Lou's hat dripped a steady stream of water as he bent over, drenched, shivering, and teeth clattering.

"Sergeant Morrissey I feel horrible keeping you out in this weather. This is not good for you."

"It's not your fault it's raining," he said good naturedly. His face had a blue tint to it.

"You're freezing!" Janet moved under the canopy of the theater's entrance, set the bag down and pulled out a blanket which she immediately wrapped around Lou. "There's a café across the street. We could sit by the window and flag a taxi if we see one."

They plodded across the road and forded the stream which flowed in its gutter. Stepping up on the curb, she gave Lou a hand.

"The cafe's closed," Lou said before Janet could turn around. Indeed, no light welcomed them inside and a small sign on the door confirmed Lou's observation.

"Oh, good grief!" Janet moaned.

"Maybe this fella knows how we can get a cab." Lou nodded at a figure approaching them. An old man with a white beard, black leather gloves and a pipe in his hand walked a very large black dog. The two seemed friendly enough.

"Good evening," Lou began the conversation. "Any idea where I might find a taxi?"

The man regarded each of them carefully. "Americans?"

"From the hospital," Janet explained.

"You didn't hear?"

"Hear what?"

"The Petworth taxis have been commissioned on an emergency run to Worthing. Won't be back for a while. Picking up British troops, I believe. The hospital, eh? A bit of a walk from here. Looks as though you're stranded." His smile twisted a little.

"I don't suppose you know how we could get back to the base. I don't mind walking, but this soldier would have trouble in the mud ..."

He shook his head. "No, ma'am. I don't own a vehicle, and most of those who do around here donated theirs for the war effort. You might wait for the officer that owns that Humber to leave town. That's the most help I can be for you." His dog pulled at the leash. The man adjusted his hat, puffed on his pipe and nodded a goodbye.

"Well! That's dandy," Janet complained. "What are we going to do? You need to be in a warm bed and I need to get back for duty."

"Calm down. We'll make it back before dark." Sergeant Morrissey stepped off the curb and with a nod, invited her to join him.

"You can attest to that?" she asked. He offered his arm while leaning on his crutches, and adjusted the blanket around his shoulders with his other hand. His strength and fortitude astounded her. She slipped her arm through his.

"If we must, we can walk back to camp. It's not all that far," he offered

"Not in this downpour, you won't. I'll be court-martialed if you catch pneumonia."

He laughed, his grin wide, and the twinkle in his eye brighter than the street lamps. "I won't catch pneumonia, and no one is going to court-martial you, even if I do get sick."

"Oh, you don't know that! I happen to have a commanding officer who—" She thought twice about saying any more. "Well, he's not happy with me right now."

"Is that right?" Lou's inquiry seemed more than idle curiosity. "It wouldn't have anything to with Lieutenant Frost, would it?"

Janet stopped for a minute. "What do you know?"

"Just what I overheard. I don't sleep all that soundly. And the doctors aren't all that quiet. Besides, that little escapade of leaving the officers' dance made me suspicious. What I don't understand is what Major Billet has against you and Lieutenant Frost being together."

"We're not together."

They reached the other side of the street again, and Lou rested his crutches against a bench by a shop window. "If you take another blanket out of that bag, we'll have a dry place to sit. And then you can tell me what's going on. Don't be elusive. You can trust me. I'm not going to start any rumors nor will I in any way make life hard for you."

"Why are you so concerned?"

"Because you're too sweet a lady to have your heart broken."

"You're making too many assumptions." Janet sat down on the blanket she had spread across the bench, and folded her hands on her lap. "There are things you aren't aware of." She had no intentions of telling him her problems.

He lowered himself carefully next to her, stretched out his wounded leg, and rubbed his knee.

"Then please, make me aware."

"And why would I tell an infantry man about my personal challenges?" She watched him struggle for an answer.

His expression half mischievous, he rolled his tongue in his cheek, and then rubbed his knee again before he answered. "Maybe," he began, pausing briefly. "Maybe because this infantryman hasn't anything better to do than to be an understanding ear. A shoulder to cry on, if you will."

"Cry?" Did she need a shoulder to cry on? She certainly needed to vent but who was there to understand? She refused to drag Marty and Sue into a drama they didn't need, and any gossip could get back to Major Billet. His threats were real. With the snap of his fingers she would be headed to Burma.

She watched the rain drip off the corners of the canvas overhang, bounce onto the cobblestones, and trickle as a steady stream into the gutters. "Promise not to tell anyone?"

"I swear a soldier's oath."

She trusted him. What would he gain by spreading rumors? She drew a deep breath. This was a good time to talk about her difficulties—in the rain with someone gentle and kind and who would probably be sent home sooner than later. "Alright then, I'll tell you. Major Billet thinks Frost and I are having an affair, but we're not. Lieutenant Frost is married and loves his wife. He would never do anything to hurt her."

"I gathered that much from the conversations I overheard."

"Because we walked to the dance together, and Major Billet saw us having a drink, his assumed his suspicions were validated. Now, a transfer to CBI hangs over Frost's head. The major informed me the night of the dance that if I continue to have a relationship with Frost, which I don't, then he'd send him to Burma. All because of me! So now I can't even talk to him except on a professional level."

"So, you've cut off all communication with him."

"Yes."

Lou grunted and sat upright. "Seems a little extreme. Why is Major Billet so concerned about Frost's love life?"

Janet stared at him, unsure whether she could even tell him the answer. But the issue had been swelling inside of her like an infection coming to a head. She bit her tongue to keep from blurting the truth.

Morrissey sat quiet, staring at her. "Why?" he asked again. "What is it?" he asked, his voice as gentle and understanding as Father Dean's forgiveness had been.

"Major Billet wants ..." She couldn't say it. She looked away.

"You?" he whispered.

She didn't answer, but she didn't need to.

"I'm sorry."

When she faced him again, he wiped a tear from her eye with his thumb. His touch so gentle and caring that it caused more tears to swell.

"Jealousy, that dragon which slays love under the pretense of keeping it alive," he whispered.

She recognized the quote and was glad she had a distraction. "Havelock Ellis wrote that. An English physician and supporter of women's rights."

"Sorry to say, he was born before his time. Unfortunately, men aren't quick to change, even during war."

"Some men aren't. That's for sure." She pulled her hankie from her pocket and blew her nose. "Look, I'm sworn to secrecy. If Major Billet finds out I told you or anyone…"

"Don't worry. Your secret's safe with me. As are you," he added under his breath, but loud enough that Janet heard. The statement comforted her, and she remembered how he had defended her against Sergeant Zoey Patterson.

She let him hold her hand, his large fingers wrapped over hers, wet but warm. A fighting man's hand. Bruised and scabbed from battle, yet his touch tender.

"So, what did you think of the movie?" She had to make small talk. If she didn't, she'd fall apart thinking about Major Billet, his lonely den, and how vulnerable she was to him.

"Petty," Lou answered. "I tried to enjoy it, but aside from looking at Loretta Young's lovely face, the story made me mad. Life's too short to play such games. Why do people do that? Why do they commit themselves to marriage, and then walk away at the sight of a pretty face? Why?" He stopped himself and gazed at their hands joined together.

She slipped hers away.

He continued. "When you see people all around you die, life and love have new meaning. Loyalty, honor—those things become your religion."

"Our integrity shouldn't need to depend on seeing friends die," Janet assured him. "We can mature well enough without fighting wars." She stood and slipped her hood back over her head. "Look, I think our carriage awaits."

The officer's car they had seen earlier pulled up at the curb in front of them and a driver stepped out. Major McCall rolled down the window and Janet gave him a quick salute.

"Shouldn't you be heading back to camp?" he asked from the front seat. He glared at Lou.

"We were thinking the same thing. But I guess the cabs are on a military errand," Janet answered.

"So, they are. Get in."

No sooner had Lou followed her into the backseat of the coach, when Major McCall began his drilling. "What are you doing out in this weather with a patient, Castner?"

"It was the doctor's suggestion that Sergeant Morrissey get out of the ward for a bit, get some fresh air. See a movie."

"Was it?" His voice reeked of sarcasm. He turned halfway around, making his disapproval known by the frown on his face. "Sending a crippled patient into the pouring rain seems like an odd thing for one of our doctors to prescribe. Which doctor?" he asked.

Janet stared at him speechless.

"Tell me."

"If you read Lou's medical records, you would see…" She glanced at Lou. Did Morrissey need to hear why he had been taken to Petworth?

"I was depressed, sir." Lou blurted. "The doctor was looking after my mental health. I'm afraid I had everyone worried. Fresh air was just what I needed. I'm better now, thanks to Lieutenant Frost."

Major McCall couldn't turn fully around to look at Lou, so he grimaced at Janet, instead. "This kind of behavior is not acceptable."

He said nothing else after that. As the car splashed through puddles and spun across mudholes on the way back to the hospital, Janet worried about the repercussions to come. Doubtful that Lou's excuse would be the end of the conversation, she hoped she hadn't pushed Frost closer to Burma.

 Chapter 19

Light Against the Dark

By the time the Humber came to a stop at the end of the drive, Lou's temper had peaked. Any longer in the vehicle with McCall might have caused him to say something he'd regret. The man already had a reputation for being rude to the patients in 105. Now he disrespected the best doctor on base. Major or not, McCall proved himself envious of Frost's superior medical knowledge and skills. Either that or he was a stiff.

McCall wasn't Lou's commander, but he outranked him, so Lou had to keep his mouth shut. "Pity," Lou muttered derisively to himself, "nothing can be done about the unfavorable gossip spreading in the wards. No one likes you, McCall."

The driver opened their door and stepped back, watching idly as Lou shuffled his crutches out of the car and leaned on them. Janet followed and saluted the major before she took Lou's arm and helped him gain his balance.

"That bloke should be transferred out of here," Lou mumbled once the major was gone. "He's a dime-store doctor at best and a beast at his worst."

Janet didn't respond, and he didn't expect her to. She was too nice, and she'd get in trouble bad-mouthing her superior. Lou stopped in front of the hut and reached in his pocket for his cigarettes, popping one out of the pack. "Smoke?" He tapped the pack and held it up.

"Sure."

Lou lit hers first. Her hands trembled. It worried him. "Cold?"

"No," she answered as she tightened the ribbon to fasten her hood. "Not really cold. Nervous maybe."

"Why? Because of McCall?"

"You might say so."

"I'm sorry things aren't working out well for you. What with McCall's callous devotion to regulations, and Billet's romantic illusions, you don't have a platform to stand on. The two have you between a rock and a boulder. Hard to do your job with all that drama."

"Hard, but I manage."

"You manage well." He blew out a puff of smoke into the dreary British fog. The rain had stopped, but the clouds hovered as twilight neared. "You know, I have a friend. Jack. He used to tell me no matter what's against you, just keep pressing on. Don't listen to people who'd bring you down."

"He's right. I know. Sometimes it's not so easy."

"No. But that's what makes you tough."

She coughed out a laugh.

"I mean, tough inside."

"I know what you meant."

He shifted his weight. He hadn't meant to insult her, and couldn't tell if she took offense or not. "So, what brought you here? Why'd you join up with the Corps?"

"I wanted to do something to help. Too many nice guys getting hurt. All the women in the States are pitching in for the war effort, somehow. Nursing's my passion. Nursed my grandpa until he died. Then I thought it was time to nurse some soldiers."

She smiled at him and it sent a chill down his spine. He hadn't seen any smile quite like hers, and especially none meant for his eyes alone.

"Why did you join?" she asked.

"Jack and I made a vow over a beer. We spent a lot of time talking about things. Had a lot of good solutions on how to save the world. Then the US got involved in this war, and we figured the time of talk was over."

"Makes sense. This Jack, he must be a good friend."

"Knew him since I was a tyke. We grew up together."

"Where is he now?"

"France. Somewhere. He got assigned to a different division, but I think we would have met up in Paris if I hadn't been wounded." Lou couldn't keep his eyes off her. Such smooth and flawless skin, her perfect lips and large hazel eyes. Just being next to her was healing. "Look, I want to thank you for being a good nurse to me. You give me something to look forward to when I wake up in the morning. I mean, probably all soldiers say those kinds of things to their nurses, but—" Lou wanted his words to go deeper. "You've saved my life in more ways than one."

"I'm glad for that," she whispered. Her voice cracked a little as their eyes met. He searched hers, looking for something more. What, he didn't know. Care? Concern? Affection? She was more than just a staff nurse doing a job. She was a beautiful, sensitive human being that cared for the wounded warriors selflessly, paying no attention to her own welfare.

"If I can do anything to help ..." She laughed, and he touched her arm, hoping she'd stop.

"No. I'm serious. If I can help you get out of this predicament you seem to be in, let me know. I doubt they're going to send me back to France. Heck, I might get a medical discharge soon. Maybe they'll send me back to the States. So, it doesn't matter if I put myself out on the line for you. What's important is that they treat you right."

"I don't know if there's anything you can do, but I appreciate the offer," she whispered. "Thank you, Lou."

He sighed. Hearing his name come from her lips melted everything bitter inside of him. He swore to himself that very moment that he would lay his life down for her. Somehow, he would take her away from her troubles and make her happy again.

"Let's go inside," she said.

Once they stepped into the ward, Janet unbuttoned her cape. Lou set his crutches against the door and then helped her take off her wrap. He folded the cloak neatly over his arm and handed it to her.

"Thank you," she said. "You're quite a gentleman."

"And you, a lady." He grinned, enjoying that she blushed.

"And you the patient. It's time to get you into bed and inspect that wound. Seems you might have damaged it again when you saved me from the bomb."

"I think you're right." Lou winced, weakened by the smell of antiseptic that lingered in the atmosphere. "What is it about this place that makes my leg hurt?"

"Hang in there, mister." Janet all but carried him to the bed and after he sat down, she rolled up his pant. He took his jacket off and slung it on the floor.

Blood oozed through the wrap.

"You need a doctor."

"Please," Lou agreed. He leaned back and closed his eyes. The cold and rainy weather must have numbed him, but now his leg pulsated with pain. He peeked once at the weeping gash when she peeled off the gauze that had adhered to his flesh.

The sore had opened, and fragments of bone protruded through. "Oh God," he moaned and closed his eyes again.

Janet brought him a cup of whiskey, which he drank greedily. "No more lunging away from bombs for you."

"Or rescuing princesses?" he asked.

"No, sir. Not unless you have to."

"I had to," his voiced tapered and though he didn't black out, he detached from reality, the sweet flavor of whiskey warm on his tongue. Time passed. He moved into consciousness only long enough to hear McCall's voice.

"We'll have to schedule another operation," the doctor told Janet.

Whether it was the pain that made him weak, the whiskey, or maybe Janet had given him morphine, he didn't know. Soon all he saw were Janet's perfect red lips moving, and her sad hazel eyes full of sympathy.

 Chapter 20

Where is She?

Janet received a note to report to Major Billet's office.

"What could possibly be the problem this time?" she asked Marty after giving the messenger a biscuit she'd baked the night before. "For your troubles," she offered.

"Thanks," the soldier said and left.

"Maybe you're getting your stripes. Some of the girls have been getting promotions, I heard. You're up for one. Maybe that's it."

"Highly unlikely," Janet grunted. Perhaps the major wanted his whiskey back. She combed her hair, taking as much time as she could afford.

"You aren't stalling, are you?" Sue asked, tapping her on the shoulder.

"Do you know anyone who would drop what they're doing and race over to his palace for a one-on-one talk with Major Billet?"

"Not unless he was standing at the door. He's got a mean streak, you know."

Janet turned sharply for fear he may be in the hut and laughed when her worries proved unjustified. "Stop teasing me, Sue. You know I'm still antsy about the closet episode."

"If he hasn't gotten on your case for that yet, I think you can forget it." Marty poured a cup of coffee. "But if you don't get over there pronto, he might think up another excuse for disciplining you."

"It'd be just like him, too."

Janet threw her cape over her shoulders and gave each of her friends a worrisome goodbye.

"You'll be fine." Sue waved.

"Tell him 'Hi' for us," Marty offered.

Janet rolled her eyes and walked briskly to the old house at the end of the drive.

"Sit down, Castner," Major Billet ordered. His usually seductive voice was absent, replaced by a stern growl.

"What did I do, this time, sir?" she asked, hoping he'd be blunt and get the meeting over with quickly.

"It's not you, per se. There's a problem with one of our nurses."

"Oh?" Janet couldn't imagine who he was referring too. All the nurses in her charge were hard workers and skilled. "Who?"

"Lieutenant Dobi. Do you know where she is?"

Janet stared at him for a long while. She hadn't seen Dobi since the afternoon the girl said goodbye. "No, but that's not unusual. Dobi doesn't work in my ward very often and with hundreds of nurses ..."

"Well, no one else has seen her either."

"What?"

"She went on leave in the middle of August. It's now September. Dobi is nowhere to be found."

"She never came back?"

"No. She's been AWOL for near two weeks! Military police have been searching for her."

Janet sucked in her breath. She hadn't even missed the girl. "I was not aware."

"Yes, I realize that. I thought I should warn you that she'll be arrested as soon as she's found. What I need from you is some information. Did she indicate where she might be headed?"

"She went to visit her husband in Horsham. Maybe something happened to her. An accident."

Billet poured himself a cup of coffee and sipped on it. His calm demeanor made her even more nervous.

"Sir, honest, I had no idea her plan was to leave and not come back."

"I certainly hope you didn't! However, because you requested leave on her behalf, the Army wants to do an investigation."

Janet sunk back in her chair and covered her face with her hands. Why was she always in trouble?

"If it makes you feel any better—" His voice softened as he set his cup on his desk. "I'm under investigation as well."

"You?"

"Lieutenant Dobi had no seniority. She wasn't up for leave for another couple of months. Our superiors want answers."

"Oh, good grief! What do we do?"

"Find her, for one. Get a statement from her claiming she did this all on her own. Otherwise, guess who answers to the colonel?"

"You?"

He continued to stare at her.

"Me?"

"I'd love to be your protector, Janet, but I have a lot more to lose than you do."

Well that was just dandy! He turned his back to her and strolled to the window.

Janet stood. Every vein in her body boiled with fury, yet she had to contain herself and watch her words. "I'll find her, sir."

"Please do."

Chapter 21

Scotland

Fortunately for Janet, two nurses returned from Horsham bearing a rumor that Dobi had been staying out in the country with her in-laws. Finding the girl wouldn't be a problem. The problem would be convincing her to turn herself in. As Janet struggled with how she might persuade Dobi to do the right thing, Lieutenant Samson showed up at the mess hall. Dressed to the hilt in his finest uniform—boots and brass shining, his buttons nearly popping from pride—he saluted Janet with overwhelming enthusiasm. On his head was a beret tipped to the side.

"Where are you off to?" Marty asked as she buttered her muffin, an amused grin on her face.

"You mean where are we off to?" the Lieutenant answered. "To the most beautiful golden shores in all of the British Isles. Dunvegan, Scotland." With all the grandeur of a nobleman, Sammy took off his beret and bowed low. When he arose, his head was pink from blood rushing to it. His eyes twinkled. "And you my lassies will be enjoying my company on a tour. Along with Lieutenant Frost, Parker, Rudy, and the pilots."

Marty's eyes opened wide, and Sue spit out her food holding back a laugh. Janet felt heat rush to her head. She had forgotten to tell her friends about the trip.

"You look surprised! Had not the lady Castner spoken to you?"

All eyes nailed Janet. She set her coffee cup down. "I forgot," she said. "What with Dobi and all. I'm sorry. But this shouldn't be a problem. I'm on a mission to find someone, but I know where she is, so I can wait a day to go fetch her. How can I pass up going to Scotland? Let's do this."

"Then the carriage awaits. Look for my jeep. One hour before the flight leaves from the grounds at Petworth Manor. Bring blankets. The beach is cold at night."

Marty and Sue didn't waste any time jumping up from the table. Janet swallowed her coffee and caught up to them.

"Why in the world didn't you tell us about this?" Sue complained.

"With everything else going on, I forgot. Don't you want to go?"

"Of course, I want to go."

Aboard the Lodestar, Janet took a seat across the aisle from Lieutenant Frost, relieved that they were away from their commanding officers and thankful she'd be able to communicate with him again. As soon as Sammy ended his introduction to the pilots and their private airplane, Frost leaned toward her and spoke.

"I am not ignoring you."

"I know."

"I'm dreadfully sorry for the way I've been acting, but McCall seems to be my private body guard these days. He's working for Billet, you know."

"I assumed," Janet assured him. "No need to apologize."

"Billet threatened to send you to Burma if we continued seeing each other. He refuses to believe we aren't having an affair," Frost confided.

"That's exactly how Major Billet threatened me. Only, you were the one going to CBI."

Frost's face whitened and then flushed. "I'd report them, if I thought it'd do any good. But according to the military, being transferred to another unit isn't a threat. It's an opportunity."

Janet snickered.

The air was clear, and a golden sunrise welcomed the private plane into the sky. They flew toward the western shores of Scotland, low enough to view the patchwork landscape of the British Isle. Only a few hundred miles away across the Channel, soldiers fought a brutal war, while they headed for a coastline free from turmoil.

"Look! A castle?" Sue whispered in Janet's ear as they soared toward a small island off the coast.

"That's the Isle of Skye. Our destination. That's Dunvegan Castle, ladies. Seat of the chief of Clan MacLeod. Amazing history and legends come from there," Sammy announced from his seat behind them. "A clan you will get to meet and those Scottish lasses I told you about."

"They live in the castle?" Marty seemed less than impressed.

"No. They have homes along the bay. No one lives in the castle, I don't think. But we may get to visit it. We'll have the party of a lifetime, eh, Parker?"

"Sounds good to me," Lieutenant Parker agreed.

After landing on a beach, the group pulled their belongings from the plane. Sammy immediately began collecting driftwood for a fire while Lieutenant Frost and Janet walked along the shore with the intent of gathering kindling.

One of the warmest days Janet had seen in a long time, she welcomed the sun's rays on her back and the salty sea spray on her face. She breathed deeply.

"Any sign of Lieutenant Dobi?" Frost asked.

"Yes. A couple of nurses on leave found her in Horsham, right where she said she was going. Evidently, she knows the police are looking for her and is evading them. The nurses managed to talk to her. Dobi is scared to come back. I wish she'd realize she isn't going to get out of this. If she returns on her own, she'll have a better chance of not being court-martialed. Or at least get an easier sentence."

"How much time is Billet going to give you before he moves in with the MPs?"

"He gave us another week."

"Good luck," he offered.

"We'll need it."

"Horsham isn't all that far away. If you want me to take you there, I can borrow a jeep."

"I would appreciate that."

They walked quietly for a while. The sun glistening on the wet sand, the seagulls squawking, and sandpipers playing tag with the breakers eased her mind. She didn't come to Scotland to worry about Dobi, she came for a retreat. "How beautiful," she whispered.

"It is," Frost agreed. "I've been inclined to forget there are still pleasures in this life, being so enveloped by war."

"Yes." For Janet the pleasures were more than a peaceful beach or glistening sunset. She thought of Morrissey—his smile, his tender touch, his sparkling green eyes, and the way everything inside of her bubbled when she was near him. "Someday I'm going to be home again, and I'll have a house of my own with yellow curtains and flower boxes with red geraniums, and maybe a cat sleeping lazily on the sofa." Maybe even a husband, she thought, as an image of Lou lingered in her mind.

"I believe you will."

"You're lucky you have a home to go to, already. I hope you get to see your wife soon." She glanced up at him.

"It's in my prayers. It may not be too long from now, either. The papers yesterday said the Germans surrendered in Marseilles. We know Brussels has been liberated. Rumor is the European war may be over soon. If one can believe rumors."

"I'd like to believe it!" Janet said.

"In the meantime, we need to stay on the good side of our superiors. I hate to be so distant with you, but …"

"I know. We both have a lot at stake."

"Our patients are our top priority. Let's just concentrate on that. And speaking of patients, how was your trip into Petworth with Sergeant Morrissey? After I operated, they took me out of 105 so I never got to follow up. I heard Morrissey was reinjured. How did that happen?"

"Remember the buzz bomb?"

"The one that flew right over Petworth?"

"Yes. We were in town. Sirens blared and people on the streets panicked. Lou grabbed me and pulled me to cover. I'm afraid that's when he hurt himself."

Lieutenant Frost gave her an inquisitive stare. "Lou?"

Janet ignored him. "I don't think he enjoyed the movie all that much, but how could he, poor guy. He gave little indication he was hurt. By the time the movie was over, it was raining so hard we could barely see. To top it off, not a cab in sight. All the taxis were commissioned to Worthing at the time. McCall ended up taking us home."

"And how did that go?"

"Horrendous. He asked why I was in town with a patient and I made the mistake of saying it was the doctor's orders. Of course, he guessed I was talking about you, and he was about to wail on me until ..." She paused, taking in the low light of late summer that subdued the ocean colors, the seagulls flying over, and the fog spreading out across the horizon in the distance. Such peace she hadn't known for a very long time. Oh, how she wished the war were over.

Lieutenant Frost stopped and turned to her. "Until what?"

"Sergeant Morrissey stood up for you. He said he had been depressed, and that you sensed it. That your remedy saved his life. McCall couldn't argue after that, though he did make a comment it was against regulations."

"McCall didn't say anything to me, except to move me out of 105. Who's been treating Morrissey?"

"McCall has."

"I was afraid of that."

"Lou hasn't been very receptive to it either."

They stared at each other. Janet wasn't quite sure why Frost frowned, nor why he searched her eyes the way he did.

"You call him Lou?"

"That's his name."

"He's a sergeant. You're a lieutenant."

Janet flushed as her temperature rose.

"I don't want to break your spirit, Janet, but you're too good of a nurse to have anything happen to you. Promise me you'll watch your step?"

So now Frost was going to join ranks with Billet and McCall, prodding into her personal life? "I thought I could be candid with you," she said. "I'd never address him by his first name in front of an officer."

"You shouldn't address him by his first name ever. It's not right. The way Major Billet has been acting, he's liable buy you a ticket to Burma. How could you lead Morrissey on like that?"

Janet fought her anger and smiled cordially. "I can take care of myself, Lieutenant Frost." When he showed no sign of backing down she added, "And I can take care of my patients as well."

He turned away, giving her breathing space. She changed the subject. "Come on. Let's not argue. Friends are too hard to come by as it is."

"I'm not angry at you, Janet. I just don't want to see you hurt."

"Then trust me. I'll be fine."

 Chapter 22

Grace in the Line of Fire

Nothing could have been timelier than the trip to Scotland. What with the quiet countryside and the trip to the castle, Janet returned to the hospital refreshed.

Still, one thing bothered her. She stole away to the chapel the evening she returned to base to summon Father Dean. "May I have a word with you?"

"Of course. Is something troubling you?"

"I'm confused, is all."

"Sit with me then, and perhaps we can make order of your thoughts." He offered her a chair, pulling his next to hers. "Tell me."

"This might be difficult for you because—well, because you're a priest," she started, not knowing how to continue.

"I'm still a human being."

"I know. Maybe you do have insight. How do you control your feelings for someone when you know you aren't supposed to have those feelings?"

He sat upright. His dark eyebrows furrowed. "You aren't feeling affection for your superior officer, are you?"

"No, no. Oh that would be awful. No. There's someone else. Someone who's been extremely kind to me. Gentle even. I'm finding it difficult to not spend time with him. When I'm with him, I fall apart. I stutter, my insides shake, and I get feverish. I hate to admit it, but think I'm falling in love."

Father Dean patted her hand gently. "It's all right to fall in love, especially when so much sorrow is all around us. If these feelings don't interrupt your work or your commitment to the Army, then you needn't feel ashamed. I'm sure you can balance the two."

Janet held back, not knowing if that answer helped her at all. What did she expect him to say? He was an Army Chaplain. He knew the protocol. She sat upright. "You're right. I'll have plenty of time for courtship when this war is over. I don't plan on being in the Army forever. Someday, I'll have a husband and a family and a little house in the States with all the lovelies that I can afford."

"Indeed, you will." He patted her hand again. "Keep your hopes and dreams focused on better times to come, and on your God."

"Thank you, Father." She rose, satisfied she'd said enough.

After her visit with Father Dean, Janet walked slowly to 105 as the sun slipped below the horizon. Having been gone for two days, she wondered what sort of reception Lou would give her when she saw him again. She opened the door excitedly, only to find the room empty but for two patients. All the other beds were made, and an unfamiliar nurse worked at the sink cleaning surgical trays.

"Where is everyone?" Janet asked, walking to Morrissey's bed. There were no signs of the sergeant. His coat no longer hung on the peg above the bed, nor did his hat. His boots were gone, as well as his duffle bag that he kept under the bed.

"Major McCall reassigned many of the patients to other wards. He said they were no longer orthopedic patients. Who are you looking for?"

"What do you mean, no longer orthopedic? We had men in here with broken bones, shrapnel wounds. Where did they go?"

"The major posted a transfer schedule on the door." She turned her back to Janet.

Sergeant Morrissey was transferred to rehabilitation. Ward 108. Which meant they were getting ready to move him out. What about the surgery he needed? Janet slid out the door without saying any more to the nurse.

A breeze chilled her cheeks as she jogged to 108 at the end of the alley. She hoped tonight was Marty's shift because she didn't have the courage to talk to anyone else. If Major Billet suspected she had a soft spot for Morrissey, no telling what he'd do. Panting, she hurried up the walkway to the hut and swung open the door, slamming it behind her.

A dozen people froze and stared at her. Flickering lantern light revealed occupied beds. Several men were seated around the card table by the door. Cigarette smoke hovered in ringlets above their heads.

Marty stood at a sink washing towels. She jumped when Janet entered the room. "Janet!"

"I hear some of my patients were transferred here." Her eyes had not become accustomed to the dark, and she couldn't tell if Morrissey was in the room.

"So, they were," a familiar voice caught her attention. The men at the table exchanged glances and then went about their card game. Janet eased her way into the shadows to Morrissey's bed.

"Why?" she asked. "Last I looked, your leg hadn't healed. I thought they were going to do surgery."

"McCall sent me here temporarily. They're going over my medical records. Where were you?"

"Scotland. What's happening?"

"I don't know. My damn leg isn't healing the way it's supposed to." The sergeant shifted his weight and grimaced. "Why'd you go to Scotland?"

"Because I was invited." She sat on the bed and pushed his hair away from his face. When she did, he took hold of her hand. The pain in his eyes went deeper than she'd ever seen. "Why did they take me out of 105?"

"I don't know. I think so that Frost wouldn't be your physician." Janet whispered.

"Or you my nurse?"

"I'm still your nurse."

The look in his eyes softened, and he brought her fingers to his lips and kissed them. Not only did his hands tremble, his body shook as well. "I missed you. Not just for your bandages, either."

"I wish you could have come to Scotland with us. You would have loved the beach there."

"Someday, maybe."

His touch took her away from her troubles. With all that had happened these last few days, she had grown more confident in her feelings toward him. Fear of him being taken away ascertained it was time to tell him. "I thought of you. I wondered what it might be like to steal away with you—to walk on the beach with you, hand in hand, or sit around a fireplace on a cold winter's night and snuggle up to you. Can dreams ever come true?"

"Your dreams will," he whispered. "If I can help it."

Janet's heart stood still. For all she cared, no one else was in the room. Flickers of red and golden light from the candle danced across his face, his smile dangerously serious. Passionate. His warm hands held on to hers. He rubbed her fingers slowly, carefully, all the while speaking to her with his eyes.

She hesitated to say any more, afraid that she would fall into a bottomless pit of trouble if she uttered the word "love." Frost had warned her. Even Father Dean had cautioned her. There would be consequences. Major Billet would be sure to punish her. But wasn't there always sacrifice in the name of love?

"Tell them to me—your dreams," Lou pleaded.

"You'll think I'm silly."

"No, I won't. Tell me."

She pulled her hand away and fidgeted with the hem of her shirt. "I dream of spending my life with someone. Someone I can cherish and love. I think all I've ever wanted to do, beside be a nurse, is to be a wife. Have a home. Children. A dog and a cat. You probably know what I mean. You probably have a wife already, don't you? A good-looking soldier like yourself."

"You should know by now I'm not married." He was quick to answer.

Blood rushed to her head. Her desires were creeping up on her, biting at her heels. As much as she wanted them, her aspirations were far out of reach. She was a First Lieutenant serving in a horrendous war. He was a wounded infantry man who would soon be sent home to the States. He'll be a civilian among admiring gals, all wanting a husband. What dreams of hers could possibly come true?

Still, she could hope, because what else was there?

"Maybe after the war we'll meet again. There's a place I'd love to take you in Pennsylvania. It's a wishing well. I would love to throw pennies in the well with you. If you want to, that is."

Lou scooted up in the bed. "Janet, whatever you wish or wherever you want to go, I would accompany you." He reached for her hand again and squeezed it gently. "You captured my heart that day in the antique shop."

"I did?"

"I watched the sunlight stream across your hair." He whistled low. "The utter amazement on your face as you strolled down the aisle, taking in all the figurines and linens that surrounded you. I could only guess what you were fancying. I thought to myself, now there's a gal with a future."

"I might go back and purchase that tablecloth for Mom."

"I bet she'd love it."

She let out a meek laugh. "Then you could come with me to my parent's house and have dinner there. Maybe Christmas dinner."

"I'd love to meet your family," he said quietly.

Janet couldn't believe her ears. He wanted to know her family?

"So, you want to live in Pennsylvania?" he inquired.

"The country's pretty back home. I know places that are simply breathtaking all year long. If you come there, I'll give you a tour." The thought of exploring her hometown with him gave her the chills. Could this be real? Could they truly be sitting here dreaming about the future with each other? A future together?

"Maybe we'll be home by Christmas. It's so lovely in Pennsylvania at Christmas time. And then you and I could walk in the woods. The forest is beautiful in the winter." She waited for his answer, but all he did was grin. "I'll show you where the yellow violets grow. We'll dig in the snow and find the trailing arbutus. They have a lovely fragrance."

"I would enjoy that."

"And then there's the mountain laurel and the deer trails. They're best when snow is still on the ground."

She watched him watch her. For a moment, it seemed they were already walking together on the wintry trail. He had a twinkle in his eyes that glistened like how she remembered sunlight catching the light on icicles in maple trees. "Have you ever noticed how beautiful the sunsets are at home and how peaceful everything is at dusk? Wouldn't it be sweet to see all those things together?"

"Yes, it would." His voice was no more than a whisper, and he choked on his words.

"When the war is over, then. That's what we'll do."

This time he took both of her hands in his and kissed them. "It's a promise."

She thanked the stars the light was low, so that he couldn't see her blush. "It's probably just a passing fancy. How many soldiers talk about running away with their nurses?"

A grimace crossed his face. "No. I don't believe what we have is a passing fancy, and I don't care what other soldiers do, nor what they think. You aren't the only nurse that comes in here, you know? Do you think I make the same sort of proclamations to them?"

"No, but—"

"They enter the hut, take my pulse, my temperature. They're all so sweet. All the nurses here are charming. But no other nurse sends my heart racing like you do. I swear." He swallowed as he searched for words. "When you step through that door, I don't know. I don't know how to describe what happens to me."

Was he delirious?

"There are no other nurses that keep me tossing in my bed at night. I don't think about any other woman like I do you. I don't know what got me started feeling this way. But I do know I'm forever going over in my mind what life might be like if we stole away together."

"You have those thoughts about me?"

"I've been fighting it. Every day, I tell myself to forget these notions because how could they ever come true? You've been life to me, Janet. You light up this dark and dismal room, and you seem to do so whenever I'm in my blackest hour. I wish you would never leave."

Janet didn't know how to respond.

"I love you," he whispered.

She looked around, hoping no one was listening to them, or that no one saw the tears rolling down her cheeks. She wiped them with her sleeve. She'd be in so much trouble if word got out.

He squeezed her hand. The words she was afraid to confess slipped from her heart and into the candlelight. "I love you, too," she said.

That night, after her shift, Janet tossed in bed, thinking about the warmth of his large hands and the tenderness of his lips on her fingers. Nothing offered more solace in the cruel and war-torn world than those moments they had shared. She couldn't sleep, no matter how hard she tried. So instead of tossing and turning, she lit a candle, pulled a piece of paper from her pack and wrote.

Dear Lou,

It sure does feel good writing to you tonight. I wonder if this is going to be a much-needed habit? Even though I know I'll see you in a few hours I can't stop thinking about you.

And how long are these hours? I can't sleep. Sharing our dreams together tonight was the most wonderful thing I have done in a long time. I hope our aspirations come true for both of us. Soon.

I think the boys in 108 were wonderful tonight. They disappeared so discreetly. Did you notice? Wonder what that means.

She wanted to sign the note 'Love, Janet', but she wasn't sure if she should or not, so she wrote "Lovingly, Janet" instead and read the letter over. Satisfied, she folded it neatly and tucked it in her cape pocket. She would give it to him in the morning before her trip to Horsham with Lieutenant Frost.

 Chapter 23

Persuasion

"You're here early."

Janet slipped into the hut and hung her cape on a peg. Many of the other men had been transferred out of rehab, so only the few soldiers who remained nodded to Janet. They made themselves scarce, dodging outside for a smoke, or burying their heads in a book. Janet grinned, remembering what she had written in her letter.

"I'm headed for Horsham this morning."

"Horsham?"

"There's some business I need to take care of." She set a chair next to his bed and sat down. "How's your leg?"

"Better, I think. When will I see you next?"

"As soon as I get back. When will you see McCall?"

He shrugged. "The doctors seem to be ignoring me."

"I put in a request to get you back in my ward."

"That would be great. Then I'll see you every day?" he asked.

"Every day. Or night." She placed her letter in his hand.

"What's this?"

"I couldn't sleep, so I wrote you a note. Maybe I'm just being silly. I feel like a school girl, missing you like I do. Not sure why."

"That's odd, because I've been having a hard time sleeping, as well. Maybe we can go back into town. This time we'll see a movie that we both can enjoy. And I'll treat you to dinner," Lou said.

"I'm looking forward to it."

She had a strong urge to lean over and kiss him on the cheek, but a cool breeze blew into the room at that moment and Lieutenant Frost entered the Nissen hut. She sat up.

"Lieutenant," he greeted Janet. "Sergeant." Frost nodded to Lou.

"Good morning, Lieutenant, sir." Lou saluted.

"How's the leg?" Frost asked, his voice cold as he studied both Janet and Lou with accusing eyes.

"Better, I think. We were making plans for when I can get up and about again. I think I need some exercise."

"What did McCall say about that?"

"He's not been around for a couple of days. Seems I'm kind of on my own over here. Said something about surgery."

Frost relaxed and ran his fingers through his hair. "Well, that's not right. He should be checking up on your condition."

"I hope that transfer comes through in the next couple of days." Janet stood and took her cape off the peg. "Hang on to your hat, Sergeant. We'll take care of you."

"Transfer? Back to 105? Good idea. We aren't done with you yet, Morrissey," Frost agreed. "I'll put in a request also. I don't think Billet would have a problem with it once he sees your records," he added.

"You think?" Janet inquired, wondering what change might have come over the major.

"I'll explain on our way to Horsham. In the meantime, Sergeant, hang in there. Your welfare is top priority."

"Thank you, sir," Lou saluted.

"See you soon," Janet told Lou as she shut the door. He blew her a kiss.

Janet jogged to keep up with the lieutenant's long-legged stride. "You're on speaking terms with Major Billet?"

"I had to request a jeep to take you to Horsham."

"And he wasn't angry? I mean the two of us going off together?"

"He was more upset about Dobi. He thinks you'll be able to convince her to come back."

"I sure hope so."

"Just use that sweet loving charm of yours, Janet. It seems to work on everyone."

She thought he might be being facetious, but his wink and grin told her otherwise.

"Well, I'm not sure how you managed to charm Billet to lend you a jeep."

"I had a mediator. Sammy's headed that way. We'll be dropping him off at Worthing and picking him up on our way home. It's only half an hour out of our way. But I need you to round up some rations for us. Sammy wants to have a little barbecue on the beach before we come home. Think you can arrange that?"

"Sure," Janet stopped in her tracks. "Now?"

"We'll leave in half an hour."

Janet hurried to her hut, certain there was nothing there to bring aside from a dozen eggs. She packaged them up in a haversack along with a tin skillet and then headed for the mess hall. Supplies had been delivered only a few hours earlier so there'd be ice and with luck, she could grab something decent to eat before the cooks missed it.

Sammy carried the entire conversation, ranting about how the Scottish ladies swooned over him like no tomorrow, and wondering why the American girls were so shy. "Pretty, but shy," he said.

Janet laughed and exchanged a glance with Frost.

"You've got to come out of your shell, Castner, or the GIs will all be colonizing Scotland after the war! Won't be a single soldier left for you American gals."

"I only need one, Sammy. I'm sure there will be some picking's left over for us introverted Americans."

The lightheartedness left them as they entered the borough of Worthing. Military trucks lined the streets, and a fence barricaded the beach with barbed wire. Sammy leaned over Frost's shoulder. "That classy building to our left is the Beach Hotel, headquarters of the 15th Scottish Division. Just leave me off on the corner and I'll walk. Road's closed ahead. When will you be coming back?"

"I don't know. Maybe sixteen hundred."

"There's a little beach south of here. Quiet. Instead of taking the fork to Worthing from Horsham, turn left and follow the gravel road until you come to the sea. It dead ends. Can't miss us."

"Got it!" Frost assured him. When Sammy jumped out, Frost saluted and did a u-turn.

It hadn't been difficult to find Dobi's in-laws, in whose hands her husband had been discharged. Lieutenant Agnes had given Janet excellent directions to the cottage. Both Janet and Frost rode through the rural countryside quietly. Sheep grazed in pastures, oak trees scattered golden leaves over the roads, their wide branches shadowed the rolling hills as if they reigned as mystical guardians of an empire. The scenery was everything Janet had imagined rural England to be. She breathed in the fresh air. Were it not for three spitfires suddenly appearing out of the clouds, she'd have forgotten there was a war going on.

"No wonder Dobi doesn't want to come back," she said.

"Yes, well …" Frost started. "The idea is to put yourself in a mind frame that will convince her to turn herself in, not to give her an excuse to run off."

"I know."

Easier said than done. What do you tell someone who's running away from her fears? Who only wants to be home with her husband? She understood Dobi's motives all too well. Janet would give anything to have a husband and be home with him in a cozy house in her hometown in Pennsylvania. And if her sweetheart was wounded, or even blind like Joey might be, she'd be just as inclined to stay by his side. But she'd never desert. Dobi was going about it all wrong.

"I know," she repeated. "It's up to me to convince Dobi to march back to the hospital, turn herself in, and report to Major Billet. Not something I would want to do either. This is going to take some pretty tough talk!"

"I can help, if you want."

Janet didn't answer. She'd rather be riding through this serene landscape in silence than think about what might happen to the young nurse if she didn't get through to her.

"Tell her she's going to be found. She can't run forever. And if MPs come to get her, it's not going to be pretty. She'll be court-martialed and then dishonorably discharged. She's looking at a few years in prison at the least. Military prison is a whole lot worse than civilian prison. She won't be seeing her husband, you can bet on it. A dishonorable discharge will hinder her from ever getting decent work once she is released. If she knows what's good for her, she'll ride home with us."

"You're convincing," Janet said. "Why don't you tell her?"

Frost grunted and turned the jeep down a narrow driveway. "I'll let you have first crack."

A large timber-framed, thatched farmhouse stood beyond a hedgerow overgrown with ivy. Chickens scurried from their path, and in the distance Land Girls tilled the field.

"Are you coming in with me?" Janet asked.

"Of course. But I'll let you talk to Dobi alone. Maybe I'll visit Joey, see what kind of medical care he's had."

"That'd be kind of you."

Janet used the clapper to knock on the hardwood door. A handsome elderly woman, clad in a faded cotton dress covered with an apron—her gray hair tied back in a bun— opened the door and greeted them with a frown.

"Good morning, ma'am," Janet began. "I'm Lieutenant Castner from the American Red Cross, and this is Lieutenant Frost. We're here to speak with Lieutenant Jennifer Dobi."

"Don't know a Lieutenant Dobi." She was about to close the door.

"It's all right, grandmother. I know these people. I've been expecting them," someone called from another room.

The woman left the door open and walked away without a smile or a welcome. Janet stepped inside to the fragrance of freshly baked bread and soup cooking on the wood-burning stove. They'd been driving for a good hour or more without even a snack, so ignoring the savory aromas was a struggle.

"Up here," Dobi called from atop a stairwell. When Janet and Frost climbed the stairs and joined her, Dobi opened a bedroom door.

Appearing much like a mummy—wrapped in a thick layer of gauze with only slits for his eyes, nose, and mouth to show through and his hands swathed in white linen—Joey lay motionless on the bed. Janet stared at him in silence, as did Frost. Morning sun filtered through the curtains and brightened his bed.

Dobi broke the silence. "Can't seem to do anything else except just change his bandages every day. I pray a lot. That's about it."

Janet peered at Frost.

"No, I don't suppose there's anything else you can do," he whispered.

"Dobi, I need to talk to you." Janet spoke softly.

"I know. I'm in trouble. But can you blame me for staying here?" Her eyes were filled with tears—more of anger than remorse. "Damn Army always pulling and tugging you this way and that way. Owning you. Thinking you belong to them. Everything you have is theirs. Your life! Look at him." She threw her arms up and gestured toward Joey. "Your life. Even your soul. I hate it, Lieutenant. I hate them. Look what they did to Joey!"

Janet cleared her throat. "We should go somewhere quiet to talk, Dobi. Don't do this in front of Joey."

For an answer, Dobi grabbed her coat from the closet and glared at Janet on her way out of the room.

"I'll stay here," Frost uttered as she followed Dobi.

The kitchen door slammed. Janet reopened it again and followed the girl into the fields behind the house. By the time she reached her, Dobi had found a log under an oak tree. With her head buried in her hands, she sobbed. Janet sat down next to her, wanting to offer words of comfort, and yet anger prevented her from doing so.

"I can't tell you I agree with everything the Army does," Janet started.

"Then why did you even come here? Why don't you just leave me alone?"

"Because I care about you."

Dobi snickered and spat on the ground. "Right. Just like everyone else does. Care that I'm back at the hospital cleaning bloody sheets and scrubbing surgical tools."

Janet took a deep breath. The sky was clear blue. The air crisp and clean. Far in the distance, along the rolling green countryside, cows grazed peacefully. "It's almost a fantasy world here." A laugh escaped her lips. "There's no sign anywhere that a war's going on."

"The planes fly over. Horsham was bombed not long ago." Dobi groaned and sat up. "And looking at Joey, you sure as a dog know there's a war going on. I'm not living in a fantasy world." Her defense was hostile. She glared at Janet with red eyes.

"You are if you think you can stay here indefinitely. Regardless of how you view the military, you're in it. And you're not getting out by walking away."

"I know it." Dobi set her jaw. "You aren't telling me anything I don't know."

"Then come back with us and turn yourself in. Today. Before it's too late. Right now, you're AWOL. If you wait, you'll be a deserter and they'll send a squad out here to arrest you."

She shook her head vigorously. "I'm not leaving Joey until we can at least take off the bandages. It's not right. I don't want to remember him like—" she waved her arms toward the house. "—like that." Tears rolled down her cheeks. "Why can't you understand that?"

"I understand you're upset, but you're going to have to put those feelings aside. You don't have long. Major Billet gave you one week from yesterday. Then it's all over for you. You do know what they do to deserters during war time, don't you?"

Dobi picked up a stone from the ground, tossed it in the air, and caught it again.

"Do you want to go to jail?"

"No." She threw the stone at a tree. A clump of bark fell to the ground when it hit.

Janet's patience wore thin. She had half a mind to pick the girl up by her collar and drag her to the jeep, but she knew that wouldn't work. She remembered Frost's advice, replacing her own ragged emotions with his wisdom. "With a dishonorable discharge and a court-martial, you won't be able to get work when the war's over."

"I know," Dobi interrupted.

"I doubt you'd be seeing Joey for a very long time, as well."

"I know that, too."

She sighed heavily. "Then what are you thinking?"

"Tuesday."

"Tuesday what?"

"I'll come back Tuesday. On my own. I don't want to go back with you."

Janet couldn't imagine why going back with her and Lieutenant Frost would be a problem, but maybe Tuesday was a fair enough pact. "All right. Tuesday then." She stood. Dobi remained seated on the log covering her face with her hands. "After Tuesday, you'll …"

"I'll be there Tuesday. You can tell your major."

She obviously didn't want to talk anymore. Janet walked back to the house by herself and met Lieutenant Frost out by the jeep. "Let's go."

"What?" he asked as he hopped into the driver's seat. "No Dobi?"

"She says she'll come back on Tuesday."

"Great."

"I think we can trust her."

"Do you? Could we trust her before?"

Janet sighed long and hard, keeping an eye on the girl still hunched over like a rag doll under the oak tree. "No. But what are we going to do? Drag her back to the hospital and tell the major she volunteered to return?"

"Should I talk to her?"

"I said everything you would have."

Frost started the engine. "Mission unaccomplished?"

Janet had no idea if she got through to Dobi or not. "Why Tuesday, I wonder?" she muttered as Frost took the jeep down the driveway.

Janet had a queasy feeling about Dobi's situation for the entire ride back to Worthing. Being forced to pull over to the side of the road for a caravan of tanks did little to soothe her anxiety. The wait for their passage was long and dusty. Lieutenant Frost showed signs of angst as well, though the words they exchanged were few.

"What do you think Billet will do when we come back without her?" she asked.

Frost shook his head and stared at the grizzly armory rattling by. Not until the caravan passed did he speak. "We'll be eating their dust all the way to Worthing," he mumbled. "Might as well wait here for a while." He peered at her. "He won't be happy. He'll be less pleased if she doesn't show up Tuesday. I'm not sure how to convince him that we can trust her. Any ideas?"

Janet sat back against the seat, her arms folded across her chest. "Not offhand, unless we explain how bad off her husband is. If only she gave me a reason why she's waiting until Tuesday. Maybe he has surgery this weekend or something."

"I think the poor kid has had all the surgery he can take," Frost said. "Is she religious?"

"She's Catholic, yes."

"Then maybe she just wants to go to Mass in Horsham before she comes back."

"That'd make sense," Janet agreed.

Frost nodded in affirmation and started the engine.

Wind came in from the east, blowing sand in their faces. Frost drove the jeep to the end of the dirt road as Sammy had suggested, and parked next to a Canadian military truck. Janet pulled her duffel out of the back and slung it over her shoulder.

Long reedy grass shimmered in the mid-afternoon sun. White sands stretched far into the distance, the low tide but a whisper of rumbling white. Whether the sound came from the waves, the wind, or military maneuvers in Worthing, Janet couldn't tell, but a low rumble disturbed the serenity of the seascape. A stream of smoke drifted into the sky from a campfire not far away. Sammy and another man stood next to it.

"I thought you'd be here an hour ago." Sammy greeted them with a wide grin.

"We came as directly as we could." Janet hoped he wouldn't inquire about Dobi, what with a stranger listening in. Sammy glanced toward the jeep and then their eyes met. Janet shook her head. To her relief, he said nothing about their missing passenger.

"Let me introduce an old friend of mine, Colonel Reinhardt. We were in Burma together, only he got out faster than I did, the dog!"

The Colonel nodded a greeting. "Sam, now that your friends are here, I'm going to take off. It's been good seeing you again." He saluted, pivoted around and jogged to the jeep.

"Well he didn't stay long," Janet said.

"I think he was getting antsy. Said we shouldn't be making a fire on the beach, but heck, I'm cold."

"No fire? Why not?" Frost asked, and Sammy shrugged.

"Well, we don't have a lot of time either," Janet informed him. "I need to be back at the base for duty tonight, so if you don't mind, I'll pan fry these steaks and poach the eggs now." She knelt next to her bag and pulled out a food thermos and her canteen.

"Did I hear you right, Janet? Steak and eggs?"

"Marty bought the eggs from a farmer in town yesterday."

"I'm afraid to ask about the steaks," Frost said.

"I got them from the mess hall." She squinted up at him, as smoke blew at her and burned her eyes.

"Aren't they for Major Billet's officer's party?"

"Not these," she answered and then gave him a grin. "Looks like you and I will have to skip our steaks at the party."

He raised his brow. "If we haven't been demoted by then."

Janet laughed as she poured water into the tin and set it on the coals. She lay the steaks into a frying pan. Sammy grabbed the handle and balanced the pan on some rocks.

"You did good, girl," he said, laughing. "What do you want to bet the major won't even miss these steaks?"

As she splashed drops of water over the eggs with a spoon, she watched them carefully. So much so she didn't hear the rumble of engines until Sammy whistled low.

"Oh boy," he declared.

Five tanks rolled across the sands near enough that Janet stood, ready to move out of the way. Fortunately, a gunner sat atop the tank and spotted them, otherwise they might have been run over. The gunner spoke into his radio, and the tanks circled around them, and then stopped.

"What's going on?"

"Must have smelled the meat cooking," Sammy said and then waved. "Howdy!"

Frost took a step back as three soldiers emerged and took a low ready position. An officer appeared, eyed them critically, and then advanced. Janet, Frost and Sammy all saluted. Sammy had lost his grin.

"What are your names?" the officer asked, his expression none too friendly. They answered one by one. Janet's voice trembled slightly, as none of the soldiers let their guard down. Finally, the officer spoke.

"One of our guards saw your smoke and feared there might be an invasion. It's a good thing we investigated before we fired, wouldn't you say?"

Sammy apologized, and Frost kicked out the fire. Janet wrapped the steaks in a towel and made egg sandwiches on toast. The officer walked away and soon the tanks clattered over the beach back to Worthing.

"Let's go," Janet said as she slung her pack over her back. "We can eat on the way home."

Today had not been a good day.

They arrived at the hospital a little before sunset. Janet stormed to her barracks. Though she would have liked to have hidden away in her bed and forgotten that the day even happened, she had duties to perform. She unpacked, put on her work clothes and headed for 105.

When Janet opened the door, Sue greeted her with a questioning frown. "Well?"

"Well?" Janet repeated.

"What happened?"

"What didn't happen? Between being rebuffed by a runaway, choking on dust from a caravan of tanks, and getting assailed by allied soldiers, I wouldn't know where to start."

Sue's wide-mouth reaction struck Janet as comical.

"Shut your mouth, Sue, or you'll catch a fly."

"Assailed by allied forces?"

"Tanks. On the beach. They thought we were invaders."

"Good grief! You must tell me this story! And where is Dobi?"

"She didn't come back, so the trip was hardly worth the effort. What's going on here?"

"Not much. Our two patients are asleep."

"Two? That's it?"

Sue crossed her arms and leaned against the sink. "What's up, Janet? Tell me what kind of trouble you got into today. By the way, Major Billet knows his steaks are missing."

Janet groaned. "Does he know I took them?"

"I doubt it, but he's mad at the whole camp and is threatening to put us all on rations if someone doesn't confess."

"Guess I'll confess then. He'll be even more angry if Dobi doesn't show up Tuesday."

"How did that happen? Did you even find her?"

"Oh yes. She's living with her in-laws in a quaint little homestead out in the country. A beautiful farm. Her husband is in a bad way. I can't blame her for not wanting to come back and face a judge. Still—"

"What did you say to her? Why is she waiting?"

"I told her what would happen to her if she didn't come back pronto and she said she knew."

"Good grief, I hope whatever you said to her will sink in by the week's end. You're pretty good with words. By the way, Angelina is getting married. She showed off her ring today."

"No lie! To whom?"

"He's a civilian. Flew out here to see her. I think they're going to Ireland to get married. Jenny's engaged now, too."

"Sounds like an epidemic." Janet laughed, but a pain of envy swept through her. Wasn't it every young lady's dream to get married and have a family? It certainly was hers. As much as she secretly thought Lou might be the one, she had doubts. How could they have a relationship? Even talking to each other broke Army regulations.

"Are you on night shift with me?" Janet asked.

"Yes. Why?"

Janet surveyed the quiet hut, the soldiers sleeping soundly, the blinds pulled shut on the windows, and only a lone candle flickering on the table. "Want to sneak over to 108 with me?"

"What's in 108?" Sue asked.

Janet scrambled for an excuse, but Sue laughed. "You have the sweets for that infantry boy you left in the closet, don't you?"

"What makes you say something like that?"

"Janet, everyone's talking."

Janet's face flushed. "They are?" she whispered.

"You know how forbidden fruit is always the talk of the town. Watch your heart, lady."

"Yes, I know. He's just so sweet to me." Janet sat on a chair at the table. Sue immediately sat next to her. "He's a lot like me. A dreamer," Janet said and smiled at Sue. "He wants very much to be happy. He's seen so much tragedy."

Sue wrapped her hands over Janet's. "We're all tired of the war. You shouldn't mistake sympathy for love, though, Janet. In this business, it's easy to do."

"Not sympathy. Why, he's had more sympathy for me than I have for him. There's something special about him. Maybe it's that he cares. I mean he seems to really care about me. And he's a gentleman."

"Well that's good. As a friend, take my advice. Your relationship can't get serious. You're a lieutenant. He's a sergeant."

"A technical sergeant," Janet corrected. She knew Sue would have the same advice as everyone else, even though she had hoped her friend would be more merciful. Janet stood. "Anyway, I'm aware of our ranks and of the government's taboos. I'm also aware that we're both people, Sue. And we won't be in the service forever, nor will the war be forever. I do have a life, you know." Janet felt a little like Dobi now. Struggling to make a normal life out of what seemed like cruel regimental requirements. "Do I really need to defend myself?" she asked.

"No, Janet." Sue's eyes opened wide in surprise. "I didn't mean to offend you."

"You're not. I'm just kind of wore out. It's been a rough day. Do you mind if I slip out of here and go back to the barracks for a little bit?"

"Go ahead. I can handle things."

Janet could not leave fast enough. She hurried into a dark alley as a fleet of aircraft droned low overhead. So loud and terrifying that she hid in the shadows of the hut until they were gone.

Even the quiet of the empty hut did nothing to settle her nerves. Thinking perhaps the damp and cold was adding to her tremors, she stoked the fire until the flame burned brightly and heated the pipe to a red glow.

She needed someone to understand, not to criticize her. How can she snuff out the fire that burned inside of her? How could she stop loving someone because of Army regulations, or because Major Billet wants her to love him instead?

She sat at the table and took out her stationary.

Dear Flo,

No one here understands the turmoil I'm going through right now, so I'm hoping you will. I'll be brief, as I'm extremely tired and need to go to bed.

I've fallen in love. His name is Lou and he's a patient here, a sergeant. He was wounded in St. Lo. So many men came to us from Normandy. They kept coming. Lou survived it all. He's a hero, Flo. He fought so hard and yet here at the hospital everyone considers him as lower class.

In my eyes he's so much more. Strong, courageous, suffering and yet he has a darling smile and a twinkle in his eye that makes me giggle like a school girl inside.

The trouble is, no one thinks I should spend time with him. They say I'm being foolish. Well then, I guess I'm just the fool because I think about him all day long, even though people tell me I should wise up.

I guess I'm as wise as I will ever be because I love Lou.

You must meet him. If he gets sent home, which he probably will soon, I'm trusting you to go visit him for me. I will tell you more later.

I love you,

Janet

 Chapter 24

Jack

The victory could only be measured in lengths of bandages and in quarts of blood.

-Ernie Pyle, Stars and Stripes, 1944

Lou read the letter from his buddy Frank again, even though his hands trembled and made the words difficult to see. Frank had been fighting alongside Jack when their squadron was split. Frank got out, but Jack and thirteen other soldiers were surrounded. There was nothing they could do to save them. They tried. Frank swore they did everything within their power to no avail. After hours of dodging shells and defending their position, they had to retreat. Jack and the others were left behind. He's MIA. It all happened somewhere in the armpit of France—somewhere near Paris. If Lou hadn't been wounded in St. Lo, he might have met up with Jack. Maybe he would have fought by Jack's side like they had talked about doing before they signed their names on the dotted line. Maybe he could have gotten Jack out of trouble.

Maybes are as good as a hot bomb smoldering in the middle of London. They mean nothing. Time doesn't run backwards for anyone—it keeps going forward and shutting out the past like dirt shoveled into a tomb—memory its headstone.

For the past month or so, with Janet's help, Lou experienced life again. He saw the sun shine again. All an illusion, he'd been wrong. Just when numbness had begun to subside, the world crashed on top of him, drowning any hope he had for happiness. Again.

"Bad news?" Ray asked.

"Is there ever any good news?" Lou folded the letter, slipped it in his pocket, and reached for his jacket. He stumbled through the dark room, limping and knocking things over. Ray jumped to his side and gave him a steady arm.

When they got to the door, Lou pulled a cigarette from his pocket and nodded thanks, hoping Ray would leave. Lou didn't need to talk. He needed to be alone. Good friends would understand, and Ray was a good friend. He patted Lou on the shoulder and went back inside.

Lou lit his cigarette, and after he puffed enough that the embers glowed, he held it cupped in his hand. If he hadn't been so numb, he'd probably be crying like a baby. But all emotions had left him.

Maybe Jack was still alive. Maybe he was a prisoner somewhere. Maybe the Krauts would let him go after the war. Or maybe they took him to one of their death camps. Maybe

Jack was already dead. MIA could mean anything, but once the government declared it, it meant hope was lost, and that officials had given up looking for him.

Jack's fate joined a million-other people in this war. Lou had been part of the killing machine. Maybe losing Jack was punishment.

Lou puffed on his cigarette again and noticed a lone figure jogging toward him. A nurse. Janet? Was he ready to see her?

She panted when she reached him, offered a quick smile, and then grew somber. He had no warmth to give in return.

"Something happened," she whispered.

He didn't answer. She took a deep breath and leaned against the other side of the hut's door. She didn't stare, and he tried not to look at her, though she was just as radiant under the stars as she was in the sun. He refused to let her beauty bait him. He moved his focus to the ominous clouds that passed in front of the moon.

"You don't want to talk," she said. When enough time had passed without his answer, she slipped inside the Nissen hut.

Maybe Ray would explain, Lou thought, although Ray didn't know what was wrong either. Lou snuffed out his cigarette and went inside.

Janet and Ray sat at the table. There were two other soldiers in the room talking quietly. Lou's entrance made little impression on anyone, and for that he was glad. Only Janet glanced his way. He wanted to talk to her, but he didn't know what to say. How could he convey his pain? And why would he want to tell her how much Jack's disappearance hurt, anyway? All he ever did was bellyache, it seemed. His pain. His trauma. His unhappiness. She deserved more than that.

He fought the urge to hide. It'd be easy to crawl into bed and shut the world out, again. But that's not the way Jack dealt with life. And that's not the way he was going to deal with Jack's death. He sat down at the table in between Janet and Ray.

"Look, I'm not doing good, okay? I just got news my best friend—he's MIA."

"Jack?" Ray asked. Lou nodded.

When Janet touched Lou's hand, tears welled in his eyes, but he fought them and looked away, avoiding both her and Ray.

"He's missing?" Janet asked.

"Since Paris. It's been months. He could be a prisoner. We don't know."

"I'm sorry."

"He's gone," Lou whispered.

"You told me about Jack," she said. "You must be devastated by his loss. I would have liked to have known him because he was your good friend. Maybe they'll find him."

Lou couldn't talk about it. He could accept her consoling him, but he couldn't say any more, and so he sat in silence for a long time, watching the candle flicker and the hot wax drip down its side. Jack's memory danced like the shadows from the candle's glow, so vivid in his mind. So real, and yet so elusive.

"Play poker?" Ray finally broke the stillness and looked up at Janet.

"I have. I'm not very good at it," she said.

"We won't take all your money." Ray laughed and waved the other two soldiers over to join them. Ben had a shoulder injury and sported a sling. Al's head was bandaged, but he was all right. He was waiting for a discharge and would be going home in a couple of days. Al pulled a deck of cards from a drawer and stacked them on the table. There were only four chairs, so Ben stood behind Janet.

"Sit down," Lou said to Ben, and took Janet's arm, guiding her to his lap. Touching her was what he needed right then. Her warmth blanketed over the cold in his heart and made him feel human. Alive.

Ray retrieved a bottle of whiskey from his pack and poured everyone a glass.

"I'll teach you how to play. Just watch me," Lou told Janet. She seemed content with the arrangement and snuggled closer to him.

The cards were dealt. The whiskey consumed. Lou forgot about his troubles. Conscious of her warm body tucked neatly between his arms, he studied the hand Al dealt him. When Janet mentioned something about snacks, Lou refused to let her get up, so Ray pulled a bag of candy from his pack.

"Sent from home. Halloween candy!" He laughed as he tossed a pile of sweets on the table.

Lou handed Janet a lollipop.

"My favorite! Root beer!" She gleamed, peeled the paper off and sucked on it. The look she gave him, with the lollipop in her mouth, and her eyes wide and cheerful. That was Janet! Always taking away his pain.

 Chapter 25

Interruption

Coins stacked on the table, the soldiers pushed the ante back and forth, daring the others to put their money where their brazen smirks were. Janet leaned back against Lou's chest and laughed as the men duped each other. She hadn't had this much fun in years, and part of it was the comfort she felt in Lou's arms, as if she belonged there. As if there were no place else on earth that mattered.

A brief shuffling of footsteps outside the hut interrupted the game. When the door burst open, Ray jumped to his feet and Ben and Al stood at attention. The table shook, coins fell to the floor. Janet looked over her shoulder at the entrance and gawked wide-eyed at Major Billet, whose eyes were glued to hers. McCall stood behind him.

Taking the sucker out of her mouth, she slid off Lou's lap and saluted. Lou stumbled in his attempt to stand and when he did, the glare that Major Billet gave him could have shot a round of ammo from an American Enfield rifle.

"Major, sir," Janet stuttered, certain she was doomed.

The major said nothing. His nostrils flared, his red eyes roared with anger, and yet the room bore a terrorizing silence. Janet's heart thudded against her chest.

When he finally did speak, his question was directed to Janet, alone. "Why are you here, Lieutenant? You're assigned to 105."

"Sir." What could she tell him? That she wanted to see Lou? She swallowed, focusing on the major's growl, afraid to look at anyone else in the room, especially Lou. "I'm sorry, sir." Janet had been in the service long enough to know excuses were worse than silence.

"Sorry." He snickered and walked past Janet to Lou. "Morrissey!"

"Sir."

"I hear there's something wrong with your leg, Sergeant," he said.

"Yes, sir."

"McCall and I will get it fixed up for you, so you can get on your way and out of here. You'll be going to surgical ward 110 immediately and we'll operate Monday. You can pack your bags and get over there tonight. Get one of your friends here to help you."

"Yes, sir."

Major Billet nodded at Ray. "Gambling? I thought you were better than that."

"Just a friendly game, sir." Ray saluted.

"Take care of Morrissey."

"Yes, sir."

He turned back to Janet. "This was intended to be a friendly visit, Castner. I had some questions to ask you, and when I didn't find you at your post—." A sour look spread across his face as he regarded Lou and Ray. "And now this."

Hurt? A crushed ego? Jealousy? Janet read them all.

"Report to my office after your shift."

"Yes, sir."

He left.

Ray was the first one to whistle low. Lou took Janet's hand and turned her to him. "This might be goodbye," he said. "From the sound of your major's voice, he's going to build a barbed wire fence between us."

"He's going to try. But what can he do? Even if he ships you to the States, I'm still going to love you."

Lou's eyes widened. "You mean that, don't you?"

"I do. I want to spend my life with you. No major is going to stop me if I put my mind to something."

He took her head in his hands, leaned over and kissed her. She'd never experienced anything so precious and so delicious in all her life. He backed away. "What about protocol? I'm a sergeant, you're a lieutenant."

"I'm going to ask Father Dean to marry us."

He laughed. "Really?"

"Tomorrow's Sunday. I'll meet you at Mass."

He laughed again. "Seriously?"

"Why not? This whole business is malarkey. These officers aren't any better than you. Who goes into the field and risks his life and limb for his country? You. Your friends. Your buddy, Jack. You're the men who do the dirty work, make the biggest sacrifices. Falling in love with you is not lowering myself, like the Army wants me to think."

"You're amazing," Lou whispered, astonishment in his eyes. "I could love you for the rest of my life. But as happy as your declaration makes me, I don't want to see you hurt."

"Just meet me at Mass. And I'll sneak over to 110 when I can."

 Chapter 26

On Trial

She'd been here before. Intimidated. Afraid, even. The empty room, the firelight casting devil shapes on the walls. Major Billet's daunting presence with his broad shoulders and authoritative stride. He liked to make her sweat. That's why when she entered the room he didn't even return her salute, but ignored her until her arm grew stiff. When he did return it, his gesture was an afterthought.

"Sit down."

She obeyed—as a good soldier would— but only because she had sworn her allegiance to the United States Army. He walked to the window and looked out.

"First things first. Where is Lieutenant Evelyn Dobi?"

"Horsham. With her in-laws, sir. She promised to return by Tuesday."

"Tuesday?"

"It's within the week of the grace period you gave her."

"What makes you think she'll turn herself in?"

"Her word, however good that is. But I can't manipulate the woman. I have no influence over her."

"Oh?" He pivoted sharply to face her. Clutching the whiskey bottle from the desk, he didn't offer her a drink, he only poured a glass for himself. "But you can manipulate me!"

"I'm sorry, sir? I don't know what you're talking about."

"I think you do. You came here bartering for Dobi's leave, didn't you? Playing my promises against me. Well, your little games can get you a court-martial."

Janet froze. She didn't trust Major Billet and his antics, but she never imagined he would threaten court-martial.

"If Dobi deserts, you are an accomplice."

Janet opened her mouth to protest, but he held his drink in the air to stop her. "Add to that fraternizing with an enlisted man, and you'll be headed home before you know it. Home in a military prison. I'm surprised at you, Janet. Really? Sergeant Morrissey? All this time, I thought it was Frost. At least having a relationship with another lieutenant would have shown some couth."

"That's insulting!"

"Is it? What's insulting is that you turned down a major for an infantryman."

"Do I smell a double standard?"

He lifted his chin when she stood and in that instance, she saw him for who he was. A hurt little boy who wasn't getting his way. All the stripes and ribbons on his uniform didn't make up for the immaturity written across his face. "Lieutenant Frost got his promotion," he said.

That was thrilling news, albeit a bit late. She held back her smirk.

"He's being transferred to a field hospital in Burma after the first of the year. He's a good doctor. His services will be better applied elsewhere. I made that decision when I thought the two of you were getting a bit too sweet on each other."

When she grimaced at him, he raised his brow. "You belong to the United States Army, Castner, and I speak for the U.S. Government. Although I had wished the two of us could have—I don't know, made it work—I still have my duties. Nonetheless, when the Red Cross referred you to the Surgeon General, you became government property. I'm merely defending Uncle Sam's possessions. So, your sergeant boyfriend will be gone soon. I want you to know that."

He strolled to his desk and pulled paperwork from a drawer. Shuffling through the files, he sorted one folder from among the rest and held it up. "Sergeant Morrisey still has a piece of shrapnel lodged in his knee cap which is causing his knee to swell. Possible gangrene. McCall and I will be removing the fragment and flushing his knee. If we're successful, he'll be fine and on his way home. If the infection has spread and festered, we will have to amputate."

"Amputate?"

"I need the best nurse I have to assist us during the operation. That would be you. I had planned on requesting your assistance before I caught you two"—he waved his hand, a disgusted look on his face— "doting on each other. Nevertheless, I need a nurse I can trust for this operation. Setting my feelings for you aside, which are now conflicted, I'm requesting your presence during that operation."

"Yes, sir."

"In the meantime, you'll be working double shifts. I can't let you get away with all these pranks, Janet. As angry as I am, I'm still deeply in love with you."

She looked up to find him grinning at her.

"I'm assuming you helped yourself to some rations out of the mess hall. I'm not going to ask. I don't really want to know. War is no time to be squawking about misappropriated steaks. However, that sort of mischief tells me you have too much time on your hands."

Janet didn't argue, nor did she confess. Trouble had already buried her in mud. No need to dig any deeper.

"So here is your schedule for the next two weeks. Handwritten by yours truly."

He tossed a sheet of paper on the table in front of her and lowered his voice. "Don't disappoint me again, hon. I can only keep so much between us without reporting to my superiors."

Janet grabbed the schedule and saluted. "Yes, Sir." She wasn't sure if she should thank him or not, so she just stared blankly at him for a moment. When he returned her salute, she left.

 Chapter 27

Bells

Father Dean's chapel bell rang eerily through the fog Sunday morning. Sue and Marty left for church before Janet did, but Janet had planned it that way. She wanted to meet Lou alone, hoping they could discuss how to approach the priest before mass.

Out of the mist, a lone figure, hands in pockets, approached. "Captain!" she greeted him with a wide grin.

"You heard?" Frost asked.

"Yes, I had a meeting with Major Billet yesterday. I'm sorry about your transfer. You're probably the best friend I have here. I'll miss you."

"I'll miss you too, Janet. Did Major Billet tell you I have a furlough before I leave to my new post?"

Janet gasped in delight. If anyone deserved to go home for the holidays it was Frost. "I'm excited for you!"

"I'm pretty excited too. I get to see my wife and children for the holidays."

She touched his arm and when he stopped walking, she gave him a hug. "I hope we can meet up when this war is over. You've been a brother to me. Thank you for everything."

"Thanks, Lieutenant. I won't forget you. I'm still here for a while yet, though. I leave the day before Thanksgiving." He patted her on the arm. "Come on, let's get to church."

Janet didn't see Lou on the way, but they were late, and he had probably left early. When they reached the little Nissen hut that had been reconstructed as a chapel, she dipped her fingers in the holy water and eyed Lou in a chair near the front. "Excuse me, Lieutenant, I'm going to sit next to Sergeant Morrissey."

"Of course."

She rushed away.

After the service, Janet lingered in the chapel and waited for the congregation to leave and for Father Dean to give his regards to his parishioners. When they were finally alone, she took Lou's hand and led him to the priest.

"May we have a moment of your time?" Janet squeezed Lou's hand and pulled him closer to her.

"Is inside all right with you?" the priest asked and ushered them to a row of chairs, turning one around for himself so that he could face them. Once they were seated, he folded his hands and studied them both. "You came to ask me to marry you?"

Janet let out a surprised laugh. How did he know? "Yes." She exchanged glances with Lou.

Father Dean's straightened in his chair and took a deep breath. "And who is this young man you're wishing to marry?"

"This is Technical Sergeant Lou Morrissey."

They shook hands.

"Wounded in battle, I see? Normandy?"

"St. Lo."

"I heard of the tremendous loss for the Allies on the coast of France. And yet, the troops covered much ground and took back the country. St. Lo is not that far from Paris."

"That's where we were headed."

"Thank you for your sacrifice, soldier." Father Dean shook his hand.

"It's what we signed up for," Lou answered. "I'm one of the lucky ones, I guess, coming out alive. Left a lot of good men back there who won't be coming back."

"Yes. The good Lord keeps watch over their souls. I'm sorry for the loss, however, and for their families. We pray for our men daily."

"I know you do."

"So, tell me about this wedding you two are requesting. How long has this been in the planning?"

Janet bit her tongue and peered at Lou. "We made the decision last night."

Father Dean's eyes popped open. "Last night?"

"We've been thinking about it for a while, though. Just started talking about it last night," Lou explained.

"That's quite sudden. I would suggest you might want to consider this lifetime decision a bit longer. Did you know each other before the war began? Before you came here?"

Janet shook her head.

"No, sir," Lou mumbled.

"When a priest joins a couple in wedlock, it's their responsibility to make certain this bond is eternal, for they swear an oath before God."

"We're aware of that, Father," Janet pleaded, and took Lou's hand. "We love each other. We want to be together forever."

Father Dean sighed and patted them both on the knees. "I'm sorry, my children, but I think perhaps passion has interrupted your reasoning. Give yourselves time to get to know each other. This is too sudden." He gave Janet a long, knowing stare, as if he longed to bring up their earlier conversation. "I cannot fulfill your request. May I pray for you?"

Janet bowed her head more to hide her disappointment than to pray. Father Dean bless them. His prayers were soft and gentle, but did nothing to take away the frustration.

"Thank you, Father," Lou escorted Janet out of the chapel. Neither of them spoke until they were halfway back to the barracks.

"Guess that's it," Janet mumbled as she and Lou strolled through the quiet alley.

"Don't lose heart, Janet." He kissed her hair and wrapped his arm around her shoulder as they walked. "We'll get another chance. And when we do, it will be the most beautiful wedding in the world. We won't have to sneak around pretending. We'll tell the world and the world will come and see us."

Janet clung to that promise.

 Chapter 28

The Enemy

> *I solemnly pledge myself before God and in the presence of this assembly to pass my life in purity and to practice my profession faithfully. I will abstain from whatever is deleterious and mischievous, and will not take or knowingly administer any harmful drug. I will do all in my power to maintain and elevate the standard of my profession and will hold in confidence all personal matters committed to my keeping and all family affairs coming to my knowledge in the practice of my calling. With loyalty will I aid the physician in his work, and as a missioner of health, I will dedicate myself to devoted service for human welfare.* **– Florence Nightingale Pledge**

Janet picked up the newspaper that Marty had left behind and scanned the headlines. The war had escalated despite rumors spreading in the hospital of possibly being over by December. False hope, she thought, saddened by the thought her stay in dreary England would not be over soon enough, and that she might have to spend another Christmas away from home. Hitler had retreated from Rastenberg only to hide out in a bunker in Berlin. Invasion continued, even though troops elsewhere had surrendered. Explosions of V2 rockets aimed at London, and neighboring towns, shaking the ground almost every day. The blackout remained in effect.

McCall had scheduled Lou's surgery early morning on Monday, however an ambulance arrived before sunrise with several badly wounded soldiers from France. Along with them were several German POWs from Aachen needing immediate attention. Because Lou's surgery wasn't an emergency, his procedure was bumped to later that afternoon.

Janet struggled with the idea of tending to the Nazis. "I feel like a traitor," she whispered to Marty while lifting a tub of water onto the propane stove. "These are the guys killing our soldiers!"

"They all bleed red, Janet," Marty reminded her, pulling anesthetics out of the ice box. "Besides, if Lou were a prisoner of war and wounded, wouldn't you want him to be treated with care?"

"Of course, I would, but I wonder how many of our POWs are getting this kind of medical attention," Janet complained, hesitant to let her guard down.

"We can't worry about what they do. We're still nurses who have taken an oath."

"I know." Janet lit the burner and turned the flame to high.

"It's a pity how borders and politics harden us against each other," Marty continued. "It'd be such a better world if we could get along."

"I suppose," Janet relented. "But with people like Hitler, I don't think we ever will. Why is there so much evil?"

"I suppose that's a question for Father Dean, isn't it?" Marty suggested as she took the surgical tools and placed them in a tub of alcohol.

Janet pushed the tray, the Ambu bag, ether, and piles of cotton and cotton wrap to the patient's bedside.

The young man waiting for surgery lay still, yet watched both Janet and Marty nervously. The nurses were forbidden to talk to him, which didn't make much difference to Janet. She neither spoke German, nor would she have anything pleasant to say to a Nazi.

She discarded the bloody wrap that had held his arm together during transport and prepped the wound with iodine and alcohol.

Major McCall made his entrance, took his coat off, and hung it on the peg by the door. Without giving her much more than a haphazard salute, he scrubbed down. Janet tied his mask and gown, washed her hands, and then returned to the table and fastened the tourniquet above the soldier's wound.

When Marty covered the patient's face with the oxygen mask, panic paled his eyes. The German shook his head. Marty whispered to him that he'd be all right, but either he couldn't understand her, or her confidence failed to convince him. He clenched the bed bar with his good arm so tightly that Janet had to pry his fingers off the iron railing. He groaned when he looked at her, and then struggled to get free.

"Damn Kraut! Hold him still! Get the ether in him," McCall growled.

Marty and Janet both worked to still the patient. With the tourniquet already set, surgery needed to commence. Marty dropped ether onto the cotton, and soon the soldier stopped fighting. All the while, her soothing voice quieted him, until the drug took affect and he slipped into unconsciousness. She adjusted the oxygen level on the tank.

Once the man lay still, Major McCall made his incisions. As Janet handed him the instruments, he clamped the blood vessels that blocked access to the shrapnel.

"Hold this one!" he ordered.

Janet took hold of the retractor to keep the soldier's muscles out of the surgeon's way. Fragments of bone and bullet had littered the area. One by one, McCall pulled the shards out of the wound and placed them on the tray. The procedure took more time than Janet thought it would. Already an hour had passed. She glanced up at Marty.

"I need more ether." Marty's voice trembled.

McCall took the retractor so that Janet could bring her a vial and then return.

"Sir, he's pale," Marty commented a few moments later. "I don't think he's getting enough oxygen." She adjusted the controls. "Something's wrong with the regulator."

"Get another tank!" McCall said.

Janet searched the room. The tanks were lined against the far wall. Hooking one up would take too long.

"There's no time," Marty pulled the mask off the patient's face, holding the cotton over his nose to keep him under.

"What are you doing? I'm almost finished," McCall said.

The patient's breathing shallowed. His face paled, his chest no longer moved.

"Sir," Janet whispered to the major. "He needs to be resuscitated."

"Major McCall, the man is dying," Marty spoke loudly, her words muffled from under her mask. She looked up at him.

McCall tossed the tools on the tray and turned his back. "Very well! Do what you must!"

Janet brought Ambu bag to Marty who placed the mask over the soldier's face. The soldier's chest swelled as she pumped air into his lungs. She pumped harder.

"I can't seem to get him back," she said to Janet, frantically trying to revive the man. His color did not return. "Help me!"

Janet rested her palms on the man's chest and pushed. His body gave under her weight. The eyes so full of fear an hour ago, were now closed, his features relaxed, his skin pale. He smelled like ether. She pushed on his chest at least a hundred times. When she tired, Marty used the Ambu bag, giving him positive pressure ventilation. His chest rose and fell. Janet watched, hoping for a sign of life. Again, and again, they worked on the soldier.

Their efforts were useless. Wearied, Janet stepped back.

Marty continued pumping.

"Marty," Janet whispered, wiping the sweat from her brow.

Marty ignored her.

Major McCall watched, his arms folded across his chest. Finally, he pulled off his mask and his robe, and tossed them on the operating table. "Take care of the body," he ordered, and walked out of the hut.

 Chapter 29

Lou's Turn

"Hey, what's going on?" Sue asked when she came into their quarters. "I went to town this morning and bought us some goodies. Plus, I stopped at the deli, and Mrs. Everstone, the lady who bakes the turnovers, just happened to have some meat for sale."

Janet looked up from the letter she was writing.

"I borrowed a couple of potatoes from the mess hall, so I can make some spam hash for supper!" Sue held up the can triumphantly, but her face fell when neither Janet nor Marty shared her excitement. "What's wrong? I thought you'd be thrilled. Don't worry, Janet, I'll cook."

Marty turned over in her bed.

"I don't think either one of us have the stomach for food tonight," Janet said, softly.

"That's odd!" Sue groaned. "I take it things didn't go well in surgery today. How's Lou?"

"He hasn't been operated on, yet." Janet looked at her watch. "1600 we have to be back."

"Okay, so then what's up?"

"Sue, don't even ask, okay?" Marty rolled the covers back and sat up, still in her fatigues–her hair disheveled, and her cheeks flushed.

"That's not fair. I'm your friend! Tell me what's going on. Why the long faces?"

"Let's just say that someone died today." Janet bit her lip.

Sue gasped. "In surgery? Who? One of our boys from 105?"

"No. Not even in the same army." Marty pulled bobby pins from her hair and set them on the bed.

"A Brit?"

"A German," Janet answered.

Sue fell silent. No one spoke after that. The circumstances were too awkward. How could the life of one young Nazi dying on an American operating table be so devastating? Asking that question seemed more damaging than answering it.

Janet focused on the letter to her sister.

Dear Flo,

Not doing all that well today. It's hard watching life slip out of someone, all the while thinking you can rescue them, and then you can't. It's hard, even if you don't know them. We take an oath as nurses to do our best to save lives, not lose them. Times like these make me wish I could just go home and curl up next to the fireplace with you. Maybe have a good cry and then read a good book. Forget about war. Forget that we have enemies. Just forget about everything.

In two more hours, Lou has surgery. Sure hope things go better for him.

On another note, word here has it that the European Theater won't take new nurses. They say our war will be over soon. Several of the gals here were transferred to CBI, and I think that's where all the new nurses will be going. Be careful! Some of the fellas were talking about Burma and I guess it's one wicked place. Hardly anyone leaves there without catching malaria. All the gals here are telling their families not to get involved, so if you're still thinking about enlisting, be forewarned!

I can't write much more today. Guess I'm upset. But I wanted to let you know I got your letter.

Don't worry about me. I'll be fine.

Miss you!

Give Mom and Dad my love.

Janet

She wiped her cheeks, folded the letter, and addressed it.

Ether and alcohol fumes still permeated 110. Janet almost gagged when she stepped inside. The smell of the operating room never disturbed her before she gave CPR to that German soldier. Now the odor had a nauseating effect on her, maybe forever.

Janet eyed Lou on the operating table, the same location where the death occurred hours earlier. Her heart skipped a beat and she whispered a prayer, thinking maybe she should have spent the last couple of hours in the chapel with Father Dean.

Marty touched her shoulder gently. "Let's get this water boiling," she said.

Janet lit the stove.

Lou watched her, a worried smile on his face.

"You'll be just fine, soldier," Marty told him as she pushed the tray of anesthetics to his bed.

"You're not wearing your poker face, are you?" he joked.

"I don't have a poker face. You can see right through me. Same with Janet." She laughed.

"Then we're in for trouble because Janet looks like the sky is falling."

She broke a smile, as forced as it was.

"So, who's doing the surgery? Tell me it's Frost."

Before Janet could answer, Major Billet walked into the room.

"Good evening, Castner," he greeted her with a smile and salute. "Alvarez."

"Good evening, Sir," Marty answered. Neither she nor Janet smiled, but they both returned his salute.

"Major McCall told me about the casualty today."

Janet glanced at Lou and swore he had turned a shade paler.

"The report is that you both acted bravely in your attempt to revive the patient." He stared at her. Seductively. A show for Lou, perhaps? She shifted her weight uncomfortably.

"We're both a bit upset from the ordeal, sir," Marty said. "But we're ready for work."

"Good. Janet, I'll need saline solution for a surgical debridement."

"Yes, sir." Janet headed for the medical supplies, angry that he had called her by her first name. When Major McCall walked into the room, a sick feeling came over her. She saluted and moved on, hoping he would not be performing Lou's surgery. His malicious exhibition earlier, and his failure to help the German POW—repulsed her. She'd be happy if she never saw the man again, much less worked with him. As upset as she was with Major Billet, she would rather he operate on Lou.

McCall brushed past Janet, stopping at the sink to scrub.

"Lieutenant!" McCall ordered, and turned his back to her. She tied his mask and his robe and then gathered the supplies for the debridement. During her preparation, she didn't notice what Billet and McCall were doing until a loud scream came from the operating table.

"What's happening?" Janet asked, her heart racing.

The majors' backs faced her, and their bodies concealed Lou. Whatever they were doing caused Morrissey excruciating pain.

"Lieutenant Alvarez, ether please," Billet signaled for Marty. She quickly rushed to Lou's side, adjusted the oxygen mask over Lou's face, and set the cotton over his mouth. "Castner! Quickly."

Janet pushed her surgical cart to the operating table, which had been adjusted so that Lou's leg bent downward. Janet brought the bucket, and set it near Lou's leg. Why had they begun before he was unconscious? Was it just to cause him discomfort? They could have waited.

Lou looked long and hard at Janet. There were tears of pain in his eyes.

"Oh darling, I'm so sorry," she said. She didn't care that Major Billet heard her.

"Alvarez!" Billet ordered to Marty, who then turned the dial on the oxygen tank and began dripping the ether onto the cotton. "One moment," she cautioned. "The ether hasn't taken effect yet."

Major McCall left the hut then. For that, Janet was glad.

Marty gently curled a lock of Lou's hair behind his ears. Janet wished she could be the one to comfort him. Lou took a deep breath and closed his eyes as Marty dripped ether onto the cotton.

"There, now," Marty whispered, her voice as unsteady as Janet's nerves. "Sleep!"

Was Marty thinking about what had happened earlier? That only a few hours ago they were fighting for someone's life in this very room? Under these same circumstances? Janet's hands trembled as she prepped Lou's leg. The iodine stained his skin a gruesome orange-red. She adjusted the tourniquet.

"Is he out?" Billet asked.

"Yes, sir," Marty answered.

"Is everything sterilized?" he asked Janet, quietly.

"Yes, sir," Janet answered. Why did he ask? It was her job to sterilize the tools. She squinted at him. When their eyes met, even though his face was hidden behind a mask, she saw his snicker.

"I know what this gummy means to you. As much as I disapprove of your relationship, I will see to it that this surgery is done correctly."

Was she supposed to thank him? If those words were to somehow make up for what had happened with the German, they were shallow. If his promise was meant to give her confidence, it lacked. If the two had been anywhere else, Janet may have slapped him for insulting Lou.

She handed him the scalpel. With it, he cut the stitches that hadn't already been ripped, releasing a putrid discharge. He handed back the knife.

"Saline."

She gave the stainless-steel pitcher to him. He paused, observing how badly her hands shook.

"You don't trust me?" he asked. He took the pitcher, his steady grasp a sharp contrast to her trembling. He poured the contents carefully over the wound, letting it drain into the bucket as the solution washed over Lou's leg. "More!"

Janet filled the jug again, and again he poured until the solution ran clear and the wound was clean.

"Scalpel." Major Billet carefully cut away the infected tissue—a tedious job, as the wound was large and discolored. That done, he handed the scalpel back to Janet and took the forceps, digging for any shrapnel that may have been left during the last operation. "Ah! There's the problem! A fragment of shrapnel lodged into the bone," he said as he tried grasping it with the forceps. "Which may be the source of infection. How is our patient?"

"More ether," Marty requested. Janet brought her a vial, taking a moment to reflect on Lou's condition. Even when she'd seen him sleeping, he had never been that relaxed.

"He's pale," Janet remarked. Maybe it was because the day faded so quickly that he looked anemic, or perhaps her fears somehow slanted her perception.

"He's fine, Janet," Marty whispered.

"This is going to take a bit of time to dislodge." Major Billet's voice broke the quiet. "How is his breathing?"

"Normal," Marty answered.

"Very well. Janet, would you turn some lights on please?"

As if the world heard the request for illumination, a knock on the door and a voice from outside called out. "Black out!"

"Dammit! What next?" Major Billet growled, looking around the room, elbows deep in surgery. "I need light!"

Janet hurried to the back of the hut where the storage trunks were and rummaged through the packages of flares, blankets and rations until she found two flashlights. On her way back, she pulled the shutters on all the windows, sealing in the darkness.

"You'll have to stand on my left," Billet instructed. After setting a stationary light for Marty that illuminated Lou's mask and the gauges on the oxygen tank, Janet fixed one of the flashlights on the operating table and then quickly scrubbed down again.

"I'll need your hands." There was angst in his voice now. How could there not be? Janet found it difficult to settle her own racing heart as she held the retractor with one hand and the flashlight in the other. She glanced anxiously at Marty. Her friend stayed focused on Lou's breathing. The only sound was the hiss of oxygen seeping through the mask.

Out of nowhere, a brilliant flash lit up the hut. The ground shook. The operating table jolted violently, and Lou slid halfway off, held up only by Major Billet's weight as he pressed against him. The oxygen mask slipped so that it no longer covered Lou's face, and the cotton of ether fell to the ground. Marty lost her balance as she lunged for the tank and tried to stabilize it. The connection popped apart.

Flames soared up the back window of the hut. Janet raced to the linen closet and pulled out a blanket, jumped onto the nearest bed and smothered the flames with the fleece. Choking on smoke, her eyes teared up and she hacked uncontrollably. When she finally caught her breath, her arms were blackened with charcoal and ash covered the bed and the entire corner of the room. She returned to the wash water and scrubbed up to her elbows as quickly as she could.

People raced by the hut outside, their panic grew harder to ignore. Smoke seeped in from the now-broken window.

The door opened and Major McCall burst in.

"V-2 hit! The field's in flames."

"Then do something!" Billet barked back at him. "Can't you see I'm in the middle of surgery?"

McCall slammed the door shut.

Major Billet rolled Lou back onto the table.

Marty fixed his mask again.

Lou moaned and opened his eyes.

"I lost the ether!" Marty worked frantically to get the oxygen tank reconnected as Janet found another vial of the drug and a fresh ball of cotton.

"Take it easy, ladies. We can finish this. Stay calm," Major Billet whispered, his voice unbelievably composed—his hands still holding the wound open. "Janet, sterilize those forceps quickly and hand them here." Janet held her breath as she watched Major Billet. With a steady hand, he carefully pulled the shrapnel out of the bone and placed it on the tray. "Let's sew him up, quickly," he said. "If there's anything else in there, I won't be able to get to it tonight."

Janet brought him the needles. When the wound was cleaned again and stitched closed, Major Billet collapsed on a chair. "Keep him on ether for a few moments more," he advised. "I want him asleep for a good long while."

"Yes sir," Marty mumbled through her mask.

"Damn shame he woke up in the middle of that!" Major Billet pulled his mask off and threw it on the table.

Janet leaned against the wall by a window and watched the burning field outside. Men and trucks surrounded the fallen missile, dousing it with chemicals and water. The fire would be contained before sunrise. Her nerves would take much longer. Tears rolled down her cheeks. She held her hand over her mouth, afraid she'd fall apart if she didn't. She glanced at Lou only once.

Where the Yellow Violets Grow

Major Billet rose, untied his gown, washed, and reached for his coat by the door. He paused, as if there were something he wanted to say, and then he stepped outside. Marty remained the only one functioning with any normalcy. She wiped the blood off Lou, cleaned tools, and took out the waste.

Janet broke down in tears.

"I'll see you at home," Marty whispered much later after most of the chores were done. She slipped out of 110.

Alone, and having calmed herself again, Janet mopped the floor, took the ash covered sheet off the bed where the fire had been, and disposed of it in the laundry. She swept up the charcoal and broken glass, scrubbed herself down, and then took a deep breath.

Morning light filtered through the front window and Janet opened the shutters to see the dawn break with a golden haze. Venus sparkled above the horizon and it looked like a diamond sparkling in a sea of lapis. She crossed herself and thanked God for sparing Lou through the night. Within twenty-four hours' time, she had seen both death and rescue. Not that she had wanted the German patient to die, but she was thankful Lou had survived.

Lou needed new bedsheets, so Janet gently rolled him to one side of the bed, removed the soiled sheet from under him, and in the same way made the bed with fresh linen. He never once stirred. He had good color, his breathing was regular and his pulse strong. Janet wiped his head with a cool rag, though he had no fever. She tucked him under the covers and kissed his forehead. Would she have dared to do that if he were awake?

Maybe.

Janet found a pen and paper in a drawer by the sink and sat at the table to write.

My Dearest Lou

As I watch over you today, the morning star is shining in the window. It casts its beams on your clean white sheets, and on your handsome face. I know you must be dreaming, and I'm here hoping for your dreams—and mine—to come true.

I wish you could see that bright star this morning. The one in the South. I made a wish on it ... Star light star bright ...

I will tell you what the wish is when we get home. Together. For then it will have come true."

Janet folded the note and tucked it into Lou's coat pocket.

 Chapter 30

Deshon

When he woke up, Lou could tell he was still in the surgical ward by the empty beds dressed in sterile sheets, the medical equipment, and the cold and empty atmosphere of the room. His leg ached and the smell of rubbing alcohol was so pungent he could taste it on his lips. He moaned. His stomach churned, queasy from the ether he had been given. He was not aware of anyone being with him until he turned his head and saw Major Billet, draped in a hospital gown, sitting in a chair next to his bed. Billet's face was buried in a newspaper.

Lou tried to read the headlines, but his vision was too blurry to focus. "How long was I out?" he asked. "Have you been here all night?"

"Not all night. There was a nurse on duty until dawn." Billet folded the paper and laid it on the bed. "Your surgery went longer than I would have liked, however. We were rudely interrupted by a V-2 rocket landing not far from here."

"No lie? Any damage?"

"Fortunately, very little. A grass fire in the field and a few of the huts were scorched. It managed to cause some extra stress, of course. I did the best I could for you under the circumstances."

"Thank you."

The major nodded. Lou had never talked to Billet before. After what Janet had told him, he was surprised the major even bothered to do the operation, much less let him live. Now the solemn stare of the man's piercing blue eyes made Lou shudder. "And what's the prognosis?"

"The wound is clean of infection. For now. I pulled more shrapnel that was lodged in your bone. But about that time, the room shook, and the back window caught on fire. I had to end the surgery early. It's doubtful I got everything. That might not matter. Some men live with shrapnel in them all their lives. Some don't."

He paused, still staring.

"What do you think, then? That I won't?"

Major Billet shrugged and sat upright. "I don't know for sure. That last infection took away a lot of your tissue and some bone. Another infection could be good reason for amputation."

"Amputation?"

"Gangrene could very easily set in." He leaned toward him again, his arms crossed over his chest, and he spoke quietly. "Look, Sergeant, there are some things going on around base that I want to clue you in on."

Lou's eyes opened wide.

"I want you to take my advice concerning Lieutenant Castner. She's off limits to you, do you understand?"

Lou said nothing, but his blood boiled.

"She's a good nurse. We need her. The war effort needs her. She's getting distracted by you, and we can't have that. The United States Military can't have it. My advice to you is to let her go. Let her live her life as a First Lieutenant in the Army Nurse Corps. If you care for her, you'll leave her be. As for you, you paid your dues. We'll be sending you to a hospital in Pennsylvania. Deshon. They have the best surgeons in the States. A team of doctors will decide what to do with your leg. If they must amputate, that's the best place to do it. Uncle Sam will even get you a prosthetic free of charge, I believe. Forget about Castner and take care of yourself. The United States Army will take care of her."

He stood and took off his robe, glaring down at Lou.

"Is that an order?" Lou asked.

"Yes, Sergeant, it is." Billet saluted, and Lou returned the salute because that's what you do when you're in the army.

What he wanted to do was spit at the major's bootheels.

Two nurses rolled him to a ward beyond the mess hall, on the far side of the hospital later that afternoon. They gave him a new bed and delivered his clothes. In his shirt pocket, he found a note.

D.L. Gardner

> "Here I am in a nice warm room with a fireplace, a good book, and lots of letters to write, but darling, what I really need is you."

 Chapter 31

Zoey

Janet, Sue, Marty, and the other nurses in their unit were ordered to a drill that morning.

"Must be a sign the war's almost over," Janet whispered to Sue. "If they can't think of anything better to do with us."

"Yes, maybe they're going to march us home," Marty offered.

"Or to Scotland. I wouldn't mind marching to Scotland," Sue agreed.

They marched in the fields with packs on their backs for two hours under the direction of Major McCall. When the sun was high, and the each had worked up a healthy sweat, Major Billet strolled out to meet them with the most serious expression that Janet had ever seen.

"This is more than just a drill," he announced as they lined up. "I thought the exercise would be fitting for the occasion. A little sweat is good for you now and then, especially when an important message is being delivered. Think of it as discipline."

Discipline? Janet thought but dared not speak. She peered at Marty.

"Your work here has been commendable. However, commendable work is not enough to please the government. We need more out of you. We need loyalty."

Sweat rolled off Janet's brow and trickled over her cheek. What was he saying?

"The United States Government is disappointed in you. Do you hear me?"

"Yes, sir," the nurses chorused.

"Do you know why? Do you have any idea why?"

No one answered. Of course, he wasn't really looking for an answer, though Janet couldn't understand why the government would be disappointed in so many nurses who worked so hard to heal wounded soldiers.

"Let me educate you, then. Many you have been advising your friends and family not to join the Nurse Corps."

Janet's temperature rose. She knew Marty was guilty, too. Maybe even Sue. How many other nurses had done the same thing.

"The Allied Forces need nurses in Burma, and yet, you—you! —have been telling qualified candidates not to enlist. A conflict of interest, wouldn't you say?"

There was no sound from the nurses.

"Wouldn't you say?" he repeated.

"Yes, sir," came the reply.

"If it's any consolation, President Roosevelt has initiated a bill. That's right. Those friends and family you're telling not to enlist, will soon be drafted should that bill go through. If I read one more letter telling anyone not to enlist, you will face consequences. Do you understand that?"

Everyone said, "Yes, sir."

They were dismissed without further incident, but the confrontation led to a lot of talk later in the mess hall.

New patients occupied 105, but none of them were Lou.

Many of the men whom Janet had become acquainted with were being discharged, sent home, or had healed and been sent back to France. She hadn't been told where Lou was. Frost alternated his duty with McCall that day, and Sammy popped in to see how things were going.

Janet was especially grateful to see Lieutenant Samson, because Sergeant Alexander Zoey Patterson had been giving the nurses problems again. He yelled at Lieutenant Brenda Roland, a new nurse to the hospital. He screamed so loudly that everyone in the hut stopped what they were doing and gawked.

"You won't catch me eating this crap," he said after Brenda set his tray on his lap. "I know what's in it."

Janet had just finished giving plasma to a soldier across the hall. She kept a watchful eye on Zoey while bandaging her patient's arm. When Zoey threw the tray of food onto the floor, Janet rushed to Brenda's side.

"And you!" Zoey pointed at Janet before she said could say anything, even before she could help Brenda pick up the tray and the food that had had spilled across the aisle. "Don't you be giving me any orders. Your lover boy isn't here to defend you and I don't take orders from dames. Not on your life. I've seen you around here bossing the men. Who do you think you are?"

That's when Sammy made a bold entrance into the hut and walked right up to Zoey. With one sweep of his arm, he pulled the covers off him. "Get up, soldier!" he ordered. "Lieutenant Roland, stop what you're doing and let this sergeant clean up his own mess."

"Yes, sir," Brenda said, quickly backing away.

"Mop this up, Sergeant. And be quick with it because you're going to be doing some pushups for talking to the nurses the way you just did."

The kid was half the size of Sammy. He surely hadn't been expecting any recourse, for his eyes went wide and his mouth dropped open. Quick out of bed, he obeyed Sammy like a frightened animal, scraping along the floor, picking up bits of egg and toast. Sammy tossed a rag on the ground in front of him, which Zoey used to mop up the oatmeal and coffee. Everyone in the room watched in silence. Sammy grunted and growled, pointing to additional spots on the floor which Zoey may or may not have been the cause of.

As much as Zoey's behavior had bothered her, Janet felt a bit sorry for him crawling on his wounded hip, but she dared not interrupt Sammy's discipline. When he was done cleaning the floor to Sammy's satisfaction, the lieutenant ordered him outside.

"You'll be doing your exercise in the fresh air, boy," he said, trooping out the door behind Zoey.

"Are you okay?" Janet asked Brenda.

"Shook up some, but I'll survive. Is he coming back here?"

"I'm not sure."

Janet presumed that Zoey would be transferred to a different ward, perhaps one where Sammy spent more time. But instead, later that afternoon, the sergeant returned to his bed in 105. When Janet confronted Sammy privately during dinner that evening, the lieutenant shrugged.

"I would have liked to put him in NP. The boy's a pistol."

"What's the problem then?"

"I'm not sure. I have an appointment with Major Billet after dinner. Why don't you come along?"

By that time, they had reached the major's office, and instead of knocking, Sammy opened the door and ushered Janet inside.

"Sit down, Sam," Major Billet addressed him. "Lieutenant Castner." He saluted and offered them each a chair in the den. "Care for a drink?"

"We're here on business, Major," Sammy reminded him.

"Oh yes. I know that. What's the man's name we're to discuss?" He shuffled through a pile of folders. "Seems I had the file here in front of me at one point—"

"Sergeant Alexander Zoey Patterson," Sammy offered. He sat quietly, more so than Janet, who shuffled in her chair, perturbed by Major Billet's indifference.

"Ah yes, here it is." He read through Zoey's files, mumbling aloud from time to time. "Yes, well it says here the man's recovering from a hip injury." He glanced up at Sammy, and then at Janet. "I hear you're doing well with him, getting him fixed up."

Janet didn't respond. Instead, Sammy interrupted. "It also says he's had a head injury, concussion and possible brain damage. If you want my medical opinion, keeping him in 105 is not safe. He's been using foul language around the nurses and this morning he had a fit of temper, throwing his tray of food across the room."

The major chuckled. "Oh, come on, Sam. You know the enlisted men's opinion of mess hall food. And frankly, I don't even touch the stuff."

Not the reaction that Janet had expected. She sat upright, fuming. This was Sammy's argument however, so she remained silent. Billet sat back in his chair and crossed his arms, a smug grin on his face as if their request was trivial.

"Major, sir, this goes beyond the man's opinion of what the food tastes like. He's violent. Any other soldier would have been arrested."

"He's a patient," the major reminded him.

"Yes. He is! He needs to be with doctors more versed in handling brain injuries."

"Nonsense, Lieutenant. The man is healthy and feeling his oats. Keep him in 105 until his hip is fully recovered. If we put him in the ward you want him in, we'd need to reassign some of the nurses I can't afford to lose from orthopedics. Ardennes Counter-offensive has just began. There are patients arriving daily from the front. One irritated GI cannot be the center of the staff's attention, nor take away from it."

"Sir—," Sammy started.

"Dismissed, Sam. I don't want to argue about this. That's my decision and it's final. Keep him in 105 until he's fully recovered from his hip injury."

"Yes, sir." Sammy fumed with anger.

"Lieutenant Castner, keep the nurses in 105 from provoking this man. Regardless of their attitude. these patients, have been through a lot. All staff needs to be aware of any emotional problems your patients have. Tolerance is your job. Tell your nurses to conduct themselves accordingly."

Janet's jaw dropped. He was going to blame this episode on the nurses!

"No one provoked him, sir," Janet began. "And his temper tantrums bother the other patients, as well as the nurses."

"I didn't say the nurses provoked him, although I haven't heard the whole story. So just make sure they don't." Billet stood and took her arm, moving her toward the window where he whispered in her ear. "If you had quit sniffing after that box-ankled gummy, and concerned yourself with keeping a smooth unit, these sorts of things wouldn't have happened. From now on, you don't leave your ward, do you understand?"

How dare he! Heat rushed to her head. If he weren't a major, she would have belted him. Billet glanced at her clenched fists and raised his brow, daring her. She stopped herself.

"You both may leave now." Billet turned his back to Janet and walked to his desk.

Sammy had already risen from his seat and saluted Major Billet. Janet forced a salute. Major Billet returned the salute without looking up at either of them, sat in his chair, and shuffled papers. The conversation was over.

She and her nurses were left to deal with Zoey.

Once away from Major Billet's office, as they bucked the wind and forbore the rain splattering against their faces, Sammy spoke with a clenched jaw. "Think you can handle Zoey?" he asked.

"Well, I hope so. Since he's not on pain killers anymore, he's become more and more ornery. And I'm not going to keep him drugged just to quiet him."

"Do what you have to until his wound heals. I'll make frequent visits, and don't be afraid to send for me if he gets out of hand again."

"I appreciate that," Janet said.

"I'm afraid with McCall overseeing 105 now, things will not run as smoothly as they did when Frost was in charge of orthopedics. Too bad they moved Frost to another ward. McCall never seems to be around, does he?"

"He's not. He's busy."

Zoey was back in the hut when Janet arrived. He sat upright in the bed, quiet as a mouse, but the look he gave her could have curdled cheese. Margie left just as Janet arrived. No other nurse was on duty, so Janet was alone with seven other patients. She made the rounds, taking vitals and administering medicine as was needed. Zoey was her last patient. When she took his arm to get a reading, he pulled away.

"Don't touch me, witch!" Though he spoke firmly, his behavior seemed disoriented, as though Janet wasn't the person he wanted to address. As if he were talking to someone else not in the room.

"I'm trying to help you," Janet said, as softly and compassionately as she could, hoping kindness would keep him calm. He slapped her hand away.

"Come on, Sergeant. I'm simply going to take your pulse." When she took his wrist, Zoey grabbed her forearm and pulled her toward him. He was strong, and as hard as she tried to get away, she couldn't. With his other hand, he pushed her head down and held her face against the bed. She struggled to breathe. Once she managed to lift her head, a knife plummeted toward her throat. She screamed.

Terror immobilized her. When she saw the other patients tackle Zoey from behind, she slid onto the ground next to the bed, stiffened from fear. The knife dropped to the floor. The men held Zoey fast against the wall. The door had been left open by others running outside to get help. Sammy flew into the room with a couple of MPs. Within minutes, Zoey was escorted out of the building.

"Janet!" Sammy rushed to her side.

She trembled so badly that Sammy had to help her to a chair. He sent for nurses to relieve her of her duties, all the while patting her on her cheeks to wake her from the stupor she was in. "Are you all right?" he kept asking.

Janet swallowed. Her heart pounded against her chest. She hadn't been hurt but she had certainly been terrified. She nodded, not knowing any other answer to give.

"I'm giving Billet a piece of my mind over this. You want to come with me?"

"No." She didn't want to see Major Billet. What could he do? He'd probably blame the attack on her. And even if he didn't, she certainly didn't want his pity. "I just want to go home."

What she really wanted was to see Lou. She wished beyond all wishes that she could fall into his comforting arms this very minute and just stay there, feel the warmth of his embrace, his lips against her hair. She could sure use his tender loving right now.

 Chapter 32

Apology

She sensed something suspicious when she saw the lone soldier jogging toward her hut at sunrise. She'd only stepped outside to smoke a cigarette. Still shaking from the previous evening's terror, she wondered how she'd ever be able to forget the attack. When the young man handed her the envelope, she gave him a questioning look.

"For Lieutenant Castner," he said, handing her the letter and saluting.

"That's me." She returned the salute and after the private left, she stepped back inside.

"What's the sour look for?" Sue asked.

After reading her summons, Janet tossed the note in the wastebasket. "I have to go see The Man. Again!"

"Well maybe the major should be coming to see you with a cake or something. He owes you an apology!" Marty sat on the bed next to her. "Sweetie, we're so sorry about what happened. My God, child, that soldier almost killed you. You must have been horrified."

"It was pretty scary," Janet admitted. "I'm not used to having someone attack me with a butcher knife."

"Thank the good Lord Sammy was there!"

"And the soldiers in the ward. They're the ones who saved me. I'm going to bake them some brownies as a thank you."

"I think brownies is a great idea. We'll help," Sue offered.

"Right now I have to go talk to the major and see what he's got for me today."

She grabbed her coat. "Say a little prayer I don't break down and start bawling. Major Billet has been my torture. All I really want is for this war to be over and to go home. And to marry Lou."

Nothing in the den had changed. The dim firelight warmed the gray of English weather, and took the chill off. Major Billet returned her salute quicker than he ever had before, and when he did, he rested his gaze on her. As usual, the discomfort of his stare bothered her. She noticed something different in his eyes, though. Or had she imagined the change?

"Please, have a seat, Lieutenant."

She relaxed on the big easy armchair. As much as she tried to harden herself for this visit, she felt tears coming. Please don't be harsh on me, she thought.

"I am deeply ashamed," he began as he walked to the window. Sheer curtains allowed ambient light to seep into the room, accenting the reddish glow of the hardwood walls. "I am ashamed that I didn't listen to Sammy's warning. I should have respected his expertise. And to think that one of my best nurses might have—." He looked at her. "Not only my best nurse, but someone whom I professed to love–could have lost her life." He shook his head slowly, remorsefully. "I'm sorry, Janet. I'm truly and pitifully sorry. Will you ever forgive me?"

As much as she appreciated his apology, the awkwardness of being in his den listening to such a confession overwhelmed her. She gathered her thoughts, trying to decipher the clumsiness of it all. "This is war, sir. Any one of us could lose our lives at any given moment."

"But what happened was completely unnecessary and irresponsible of me."

She agreed. She couldn't argue with him, nor did she want to. "I accept your apology."

"Do you?"

"Yes. I can't accept your love. I can't return it."

"I see."

"I appreciate that you've seen your error. Takes courage to admit it."

"You think?"

Janet saw him puff like a proud rooster. When she didn't press the issue, he moved about the room, aimlessly it seemed to Janet. The arrogant major she had known diminished into a humiliated soldier stumbling for words. "You can't return my love?" he whispered meekly, after finally finding his voice.

"I'm sorry, Major Billet. I lost my heart to a wounded sergeant."

"Morrissey?"

"Yes, sir."

"I see."

Had she made a mistake in being truthful? She hoped not, for Lou's sake.

"Is there any way he could be moved back to my ward? At least for Christmas?" she asked. A bold request, but she figured he owed her.

"You really know how to hurt a guy, don't you?"

"I'm not trying to hurt you."

"No?"

Janet bit her lip. Had her request been too daring? Jets soared overhead assigning the tension in the room to that of the war. The hostilities raged on the other side of the Channel, far more threatening than a lover's jealousy. Yet, here Janet sat, begging to see a wounded infantry man, as though Lou was the only thing that mattered in the world.

To her, he was.

Billet waited until the drone of the aircraft faded into the crackle and pop of the fire. He breathed in deeply, his frown imbedded and disturbed. "I believe your friend Morrissey's discharge papers are pending."

"Oh." She stood and saluted, ready to leave. Lou would be going home soon. For that she was glad. "Can you tell me how his leg is?"

"No. I don't know. You were there, Janet. I didn't get all the shrapnel out. How could I have? Some of his bone is destroyed and if it gets infected again, there's no choice but to amputate. He'll be getting a medical discharge and sent to Deshon. After that, he'll be gone."

Janet turned to leave, uncertain as to what would happen to Lou, or to their dreams.

"Before you go." Major Billet stopped her. He reached for her arm, and for the first time he touched her. She pivoted around, sharply.

"Your promotion has been granted. I don't have a silver bar for you yet. Mail hasn't been reliable lately, but from this day forward, you are a first lieutenant."

"Thanks, sir."

 Chapter 33

Holiday

Janet had a day off and she was going to spend it with Lou, even if she had to slink out of her bed, crawl through the dark before dawn and climb into his window. Nothing would keep her away. She hadn't seen him since that miserable day of his operation. Sue had brought reports of his condition, and delivered her letters to him. Had he been too ill or drugged to respond? Or was there another reason she hadn't heard from him? Had Major Billet talked to him?

With news that he was leaving, Janet could not contain her desire to be with him.

There was no need for her to sneak, of course. Both Marty and Sue knew her plans and with their help, Janet made an extra portion of fudge the night before to bring to him. Major Billet had gone to London, and even though McCall was still on base, with Billet gone, extra duties kept him busy in the office.

Janet rose an hour before dawn. After getting dressed, she pinned her hair in a bun and put on her cap, fixing her spit curls in place and brushing a bit of lipstick across her lips. With the fudge wrapped in a clean towel and on the fanciest dish she could find, Janet tucked her gift under her cape. "How do I look?" she asked.

"You're beautiful." Marty, still in bed, opened one eye after she spoke.

"Bye. Good luck!" Sue mumbled from under the covers.

"Thanks. I might try to take him to town and go Christmas shopping."

"His leg is in a cast," Sue answered.

"Then I'll take the cast to town with us!"

"That might be difficult, Lieutenant. Maybe you should try something simpler."

"Maybe. It doesn't matter what we do, really. Not as long as we're together."

Janet whistled a song when she met the still-dark morning. A half-moon shone high in a starlit sky, and a golden glow heralding the dawn stretched out across the horizon. Stars glimmered above. A more serene setting hadn't glistened over the earth in a long, long time, nor had her spirits been so uplifted. This would be a perfect day—at least she would do her best to make it so.

The door to 130 squeaked when she opened it. The moon shone through the crack of the entryway and cast a beam over the rows of beds which lined the aisle. Only a few were occupied. The nurse on night duty had fallen asleep in a chair at the table. Janet walked carefully past each cot. The soldiers slumbered peacefully, mouths open. An occasional snort and snore disturbed their dreams, reminding her of the seven dwarves in Disney's Snow White. She found Lou and sat down at the foot of his bed.

She hadn't intended to wake him. Being next to him, hearing him breathe, and watching him sleep satisfied her craving. If only she could sit by his side every morning, she would be the happiest girl in the world.

"I must be dreaming," he said, his voice muffled from the covers. "I see a vision of a beautiful lady sitting on my bed and she is smiling at me. Her face shines in the moonlight, soft and pale like an angel and she—." Lou pulled himself up and leaned on his elbow. "She smells very much like chocolate."

"Imagine that." Janet slipped her tray of fudge out from under her cape. "I do not see this angel." She turned to look over her shoulder, as Lou pilfered a morsel off her plate. "But I do think there may be a bandit in our midst."

"Why do you say that?" Lou asked. Bits of chocolate dropped onto the sheets as he shoved the crumbs into his mouth.

"Well look! I swear my plate was full."

He sat up. "I will find the culprit! Look, even now he sneaks out the door!" When Janet looked toward the door, and back again, Lou had a piece of fudge in each hand.

"Never mind, I found the robber!" She laughed. The look on his face was so adorable, she leaned over and kissed him, letting the tray rest on the bed between them. Their caress lasted longer than she had first intended, and tasted delicious, bits of chocolate coating their tongues as they embraced. If only it could last for eternity. He moaned softly, and she backed away with a racing heart. So inappropriate. So delectable.

He scooted up on the bed, placed the fudge back on the plate, and wiped the remaining portions off his lips. She straightened her cap and brushed her cape clean. Embarrassed, and yet delighted. "How are you? I've been worried about you," she said, as if the kiss had not even happened.

"Much better than I've ever been," he replied quickly, staring intensely into her eyes.

"I see you're still in one piece. Do you know what they're going to do about your leg?"

"Not the slightest idea. What about you?"

"What about me?"

"I heard a rumor that some of the nurses are being sent to France. Are you one of them?"

"No, I don't think so. I'm afraid I'm destined to stay in this dreary hospital."

"Good."

"Thanksgiving is Thursday."

"Are you cooking a turkey and all the trimmings for me?"

"I am."

"I'll go on a hunger strike until then."

"Better not."

They stared at each other. Janet wanted nothing more than to spend the morning kissing him, but she'd never get away with it. And she remembered Father Dean's words about not being in the army to satisfy herself. Lou broke the silence.

"I'm sorry for getting you in so much trouble."

"What are you talking about?"

He didn't answer her, clearly hiding something. She panicked, guessing what might be on his mind but not wanting it to be true.

"Did you talk to Major Billet?"

"You're a first lieutenant now, aren't you?"

"You did talk to Billet! What did he say to you?"

When he didn't answer, she prodded him. "What did Major Billet tell you?"

"I'm leaving for the States. I'll be getting a discharge, a job. But you …" He looked out the window.

"Lou!"

"You'll be here helping the war effort. Healing people. You have a career with the military. They need you."

"Stop it, Lou! The war won't last forever and then I'm going home. Did Major Billet tell you to forget about me?"

Lou brushed his hair back and sighed. When he considered her eyes and shook his head, her heart might as well have been torn out of her. "I'm a crippled infantryman. Might be an amputee. You're a bright young lady with the world at your fingertips. What would you want with the likes of me?"

She took hold of his hair and pulled him to her, kissing him with everything she had inside of her. He wasn't getting away. Not that easily. In return, he wrapped his arms around her and they stayed that way until she was convinced he understood.

"I will write you every day, mister. And there won't be a moment that I won't be thinking of you."

His frown had turned into a smile.

"Believe me?" she asked.

"I believe you."

"Good! Now, get dressed because we're going to do something to make our holiday happier."

"Decorations. We've already begun. Frost brought in a tree." He nodded toward a small spruce in the shadows leaning against the wall.

"I knew I smelled evergreen boughs."

"And I got the guys to make some decorations." Lou rose from bed, limped toward the table, and held up a string of curly red ribbons.

"How cute! Where did that come from?"

"Cigarette packages. The little red strings that hold them shut, we curl them with our fingers."

"Genius!"

"I thought so. My Aunt Viola taught me. She's famous, you know. She set up the first kindergarten in Cincinnati." His eyes lit up when he told her about his aunt, and when he held up the newspaper snowflakes he and the other patients had made.

"It's just the Stars and Stripes News. Nothing special. Something about war. I saved Ernie Pyle's column though."

Janet laughed and took the section of newspaper the men had cut around. Her smile faded as she read Ernie Pyle's coverage of the European Theater. "This was your major, the one you buried?"

He answered with a silent nod.

"This account is so moving."

"Yeah, well it was."

"I'm so sorry."

"It's war."

"Seems like that's the explanation for most things these days. What do they say? 'All's fair in love and war'?" Janet asked.

"Only nothing's fair in either." He sat next to her and took her hand.

D.L. Gardner

 Chapter 34

A Partridge in a Pear Tree

Winter showed its face in England that year. Perhaps it was the universe grieving over the loss of life that made the season so morbidly cold. Fighting in the Ardennes had escalated, with casualties being reported hourly. No one could wager who would declare victory in Bastogne, and the stakes could mean the outcome of the war. Men came to the hospital frostbit, as well as injured, and oftentimes there was no cure but to amputate. For that, they were sent to another hospital inland. Janet hated seeing those injuries. She still worried about Lou's.

Holidays used to be the most festive time of year. Aromas of food cooking. Fat juicy ham roasting in the oven with pineapple glaze and yams. Pumpkin and pecan pies and chocolate desserts. Gingerbread and butter-cookies shaped like bells or fat Santa cookies iced with red and green sprinkles. Sugary confections made from recipes of the old country. Family gathering around a piano, singing songs of peace and goodwill. Children decorating homes with tinsel and mistletoe and paper snowflakes. Bright colored lights hanging in windows, cranberries and popcorn beaded on a string to hang on a tree. Men with armloads of firewood, stomping snow from their rubber boots. Bright winter sweaters and warm knitted hats jingling with bells. People laughing, snowballs flying, sleds soaring down icy hills, skaters gliding on frozen ponds. Lovers drinking hot chocolate by the fireplace, exchanging gifts—kissing.

The only kiss Janet would get this Christmas was the one on her fingertips as she blew her farewell to Lou.

He stood in line in the bitter cold, his canvas coat buttoned tight up to his neck, yet not protecting him enough from the downpour to keep him from shivering. He leaned heavily on his cane. His leg still not healed, still in question. His hair wet, rain running down his cheeks, his neck, his eyelashes. He turned and looked at her with sad and lonely eyes.

Janet stood by the door of the jeep, thankful that Sammy had driven her into Worthing to see him off, but sorry that she had to make this trip.

What would happen to him on a ship filled with thousands of sailors headed across the Atlantic? Where would he go when he got out of the hospital? What would they do about his leg?

Why did Major Billet send him away?

"It wasn't Major Billet that did this," Sammy whispered in her ear as they watched the line of soldiers slowly embarking on the navy vessel. "Not this time."

Janet would have choked if she had tried to talk. She nodded and blew her nose.

"Cheer up, Lieutenant. You'll see him again."

How do you leave this all behind? Sure, he wanted the war to be over but not just for him. For everyone. How do you walk away from the people who need you when they're still out there dying? Still killing and being killed. They were a team, the 29th Infantry Division of the United States Army. Lou was part of that team. They invaded the shores of Normandy together, beat through the gnarly hedgerows together. They buried their friends together and honored their captain as one unit. Now, like leaves falling from the autumn trees, he was left to drift alone. A soldier without a war. A stranger to everything that used to be familiar. Turned away during winter's sorrow, his heart buried in icy snow because the gal who warmed it wasn't coming with him. How he hoped there'd still be something left of him by spring.

Lou could have gone on fighting—alert enough, strong enough in spirit to endure another battle, never mind that his leg was busted up and he could hardly walk. He could still shoot. He could still throw a grenade. Maybe he could still save someone's life.

Where the Yellow Violets Grow

The line moved slowly, at turtle's pace. He carried nothing, but his duffle bag stuffed with uniforms, another pair of boots, and rations. That was it. Lou didn't have much when he left for war. He had his parents, but no property of his own. No house. No kids. No wife. Now he had no job anymore. No best buddy anymore.

He turned and looked back. Janet had said in her letter she'd come and see him when he left, and there she was. So close and yet so far away. A jewel shining through the gray and leaden clouds. She blew him a kiss. He dropped the duffel bag, leaned heavily on his cane, and waved. How he wished he could kiss her. Hold her. Take her with him.

The soldier behind him moved, pushing him forward. Lou glanced at him for a split second. A flashing moment was all he could handle. He saw himself in the soldier's red eyes and in the tired lines on his face, caked with the mud of war. Filth that could never be scrubbed clean. Sorrow that would never be comforted. Pain that would never be relieved. He wasn't leaving the battle front. No one would ever leave. He'd take it back to the States with him. Maybe there would be enough goodness at home to camouflage his tattered soul and torn spirit. Without Janet how could he believe that life was worth living again?

The hole in the ship where the soldiers entered was near now. A few more feet and he'd be leaving British soil. One last glance and he'd be gone, leaving the one person he loved. His hope, his sweetheart. His shining star. Janet. Would he ever see her again?

 Chapter 35

January 1945

When you reach the end of your rope, tie a knot in it and hang on. —Franklin D. Roosevelt

My Dearest Lou,

I cannot tell you just how much I miss you. I wander around like a lost soul. Christmas has come and gone and while it was nice, it would have been so much sweeter if we could have spent it together. I gave a letter to a patient for you the other day. He was leaving and there was a chance he might get the same boat. He said he would find you if you were there. I hope you get it.

We had a high mass for Christmas Eve, as you know. The choir sounded quite nice. The chapel looked lovely and it was very crowded. All the patients were allowed to come. I missed having you beside me, but someday soon we will go together.

How empty life was for Janet now that the festive holiday was over. The war lingered on, the weather turned even grayer than it had been, and Lou was many miles away. Days passed and with them, her joy. How could she have fallen so helplessly in love with someone so quickly? And how could she be so devastated after his departure when she'd known him for such a short time?

Regardless of how short their courtship, each day without his quirky grin, without his needy touch, without his encouragement, her love for him grew stronger.

"Perk up, Janet," Sue said one morning. "The look on your face is as blue as the moon. We have work to do, and it won't be any fun at all with you down in the dumps. How are we going to make these other men get better?"

Janet brushed her hair, examining the frown in the mirror.

"Captain Frost is back, if that helps," Marty told her.

"I'll be happy to see him again," Janet said.

"Then put that smile back on your face!"

Trying to put the smile on didn't work, but when she stepped outside and saw Captain Frost walking from his hut to the mess hall, it appeared naturally. She locked arms with him when she caught up.

"Hey, Captain! Welcome back!"

"Lieutenant Castner, what a joy!" He patted her hand. "It's good to see you again."

"How was your visit with your family?"

"All too short, but wonderful nonetheless."

"I can imagine."

"How's life with you?" he asked.

"Fine, I guess." She saw no need in bringing Frost's spirits down to where hers were.

"Major Billet tells me you've been promoted."

"Yes, most all of us have, though you couldn't tell. No one has her bar yet."

"Mail's been a bear lately. If you want, I can give you my silver bar to wear until yours comes. It's polished." He stopped in the street, pulled out the medal from his pocket, and slipped it into the palm of her hand."

"Thanks," she said, not bearing to look at his face because the tears were welling in her eyes and she didn't want him to see her cry. "It was bound to happen. I mean, hopefully we're all going to get sent away."

"When the war's over, yes. Until then, I'll be in Burma."

She searched his eyes, forgetting her own tears. "So, they went ahead and did it. I'm sorry."

"I had a long talk with Sammy about the conditions there. I'm sorry too." He laughed. "I'm not looking forward to it, but someone has to save our guys. Say a prayer for me."

"Every day."

"And I will pray that this blasted war is over soon." He looked off into the distance and sighed. "So much heartache,

Even back home worry and sorrow have hijacked everyone's lives. There's no happiness. Anywhere." His eyes returned to hers. "Before I left, I criticized you for your relationship with an infantryman. I beg your forgiveness. If you can find love, grab hold and don't let go. Life is too short."

"Thank you. Lou's been sent home."

"Has he? Well, that's good for him. He'll get better care in the hospital at Deshon. I'm sorry for you, though. There was promise in that relationship."

"I'll see him again. I know I will."

He gave her a warm smile. "That's what I like about you, Janet. You set your mind to something, and there's no stopping you."

"You might not be in Burma long. They say we're winning the war," Janet offered.

"Winning?"

Janet studied her boots as they stood in front of the mess hall. They both stared at the ground, letting silence engulf them. When Frost spoke, he did so quietly.

"Hitler will surrender, I don't doubt that. He's surrounded and has no place to go. A facsimile of peace will come. Cities will rebuild, eventually. But no one wins a war. Too much damage has already been done. Maybe, in generations to come, the wounds will be scarred over enough that people can live a normal life. Maybe our children and grandchildren will learn from these mistakes." He stood tall and when he did, Janet caught the dauntless look in his eye. He'd been such an encouragement to her. "All we can do is take it day by day." He saluted with a smile.

She returned his salutation. "Yes, sir, Captain, sir!" Janet clutched the silver bar he had given her. "Thank you."

My Dearest Lou,

Another day over and I'm very grateful. Time does drag any more. This past month has been the longest of my whole life, and the emptiest.

"Janet, dear, you really should try and come out of the dumps," Marty whispered after reading over her shoulder.

"I should. I would, if only I had a letter from him. If only he'd write, I would be the happiest girl in the world."

"Maybe you should let go a little bit," Sue suggested.

Janet stared at the government-issued stationary that she had scribbled on and wondered if she ever could let go.

"I mean, it's not like you can do anything about him being gone, or ending the war, or going home," Sue continued. "And he can't do anything about coming back here. And God only knows what's happened to our mail. I haven't been getting any letters either and my brother always writes me."

"You should go to the officers' dance with us tomorrow," Marty suggested.

"I suppose. But tonight, I'm going to finish this letter."

"Suit yourself." Marty brushed Janet's hair behind her ears and gave her a friendly pat before she moved to her bed and picked up a book.

"Maybe he isn't getting your letters either, Janet. Maybe he's as bummed as you are. Or maybe—"

Janet waited for the 'or maybe', but she didn't want to hear what Sue might say next. If there was any doubt about his love for her, she didn't want to hear it.

"Maybe he's just gotten all wrapped up in things back home. Maybe—"

"What, Sue? Maybe he's forgotten about me?"

"I doubt he could forget you."

"Maybe he's forgotten that we love each other? That we've promised ourselves to each other?" Janet asked.

Sue didn't answer. She, too, snuck off to her bed. Janet glanced at the two of them in their pajamas, snuggled under their covers. Still on blackout, the candles flickered in the room, highlighting their worried faces. No one wanted to hurt her feelings, Janet knew that. They were good friends. Honest friends. Marty stared at her, and finally whispered gently, "Maybe."

"Well, if that's true, he's going to have to tell me in his own words, because I'm not letting go of him until the day he tells me it's over." She turned her back to her friends and continued writing.

Dearest Lou,

It's a beautiful night. I made my nightly wish on the brightest star. And said my constant prayers that we will be together soon. When I think of your love, I think I am the most blessed person on earth. If only I could be there to try and tell you just how much I care, and to look after you. I miss you. It is like a deep hurt. It gets worse and worse as the days pass. I love you most dearly, even more than life itself.

Do you remember the time you told me you weren't married? I'll never forget that day for I had fallen so much in love with you, and thought my life was doomed.

My pen won't write the words to tell you how much I love you. My mind keeps whirling around with all that is in my heart, and all that I can put on paper are unimportant everyday things. But Lou, I do love you so much. To win your love has been the greatest and grandest thing to ever have happened to me. I am sorry for every minute while you were here that we did not spend time together.

I love you my darling,

D.L. Gardner

Janet

 Chapter 36
March 1945

I hate war as only a soldier who has lived it can, only as one who has seen its brutality, its stupidity. — General Dwight D. Eisenhower

Lou my darling,

Captain Frost wants all the ward personnel to go into town tomorrow night and celebrate our promotions. By the way, I'm wearing my own silver as of noon today. It seems as though my cup is very full and I'm indeed the most fortunate of girls. I think it is a major miracle that you love me.

Your loving Janet

Work had become a routine. Janet no longer found satisfaction in the daily pulse readings, administering shots, or sewing up wounds. One lesion looked like the next, and she had seen them all. The faces of the soldiers were the same to her, all in pain, all young and confused, all trying to do the best they could despite the discomfort and trauma. She gave them the best care she could, but her heart was somewhere else.

Janet dressed her best for the officers' ball. More of the staff had been transferred from West Sussex that week, and though she hadn't heard exactly who had been transferred, she didn't seem to care anymore.

Major Billet still winked at her after every salute. McCall never lost his grimace. Frost's worried countenance became a constant reminder of where he would be headed soon. She missed Lou all her waking hours and sometimes in her dreams. Her friends tried to comfort her because they cared about her, but oftentimes what they said hurt more than if they had remained silent.

She walked to the community center with Sue and Marty under a cold, slightly windy, but clear winter sky. Thousands of stars glittered overhead. When they neared the town, voices blared out over the music and as the hall came into view, people congregated in the street.

"It's a fight!" Sue grabbed Janet's arm.

Two men wrestled in the dirt while onlookers circled them, some laughing, some cheering. Soon Major Billet and Captain Frost were in the center of it all, pulling the men apart.

"Good heavens, it's Sammy!" Janet exclaimed as the lieutenant staggered away from the private he'd been tackling.

"Get home before I have the MPs after you!" Billet told them.

Sammy grabbed his cap, dusted it on his knee and staggered down the street, giving Janet an embarrassed glare. Clearly, liquor had consumed him. The private stormed ahead.

"Lieutenant Castner!" Major Billet greeted her at the door. Frost turned at that moment, eyeing the major suspiciously.

"Good evening, Major," Janet said, none too warmly. She saluted.

"It's good to see you here. Might I be so kind as to ask for the first dance?"

"I'm not sure." She turned to her friends, but they nodded, happy that the major had asked her out on the floor. They didn't know, how could they? "I mean—"

"Nonsense. That's what you came for, isn't it? To socialize. To have a good time?" He swung her onto the dance floor. While they waltz, Billet leaned close to her, his breath hot on her neck. "I thought we had an agreement of sorts."

"Did you?"

"We made a truce, didn't we?"

"I accepted your apology. Not sure what kind of contract I signed when I did."

He laughed, as they glided across the dance floor, weaving in and out of the other couples to the beat of the music. When they had reached the other side of the room, away from her friends, he took her hand and led her to the fireplace. "Why are you so hostile toward me, Lieutenant? I have only your best interest at heart. I told you how I felt about you. I still feel that way."

"And I told you I could never return those feelings." She lowered her voice, hoping no one would eavesdrop. "It doesn't matter how far away Morrissey is, or what you've done to him. I plan on marrying him when I get out of the service."

"I've done nothing to him. The man's leg is destroyed. He can't serve any longer, you should know that. A medical discharge is protocol under the circumstances. And you can't blame me for that."

She looked him in the eye as he handed her a glass of whiskey. "No. I can't blame that on you."

"Then why are you so angry with me?"

Why? She asked herself as she studied him. She wanted to be angry with him. Did there have to be any other reason?

"I'd like to be friends, Lieutenant Castner. There's too much work here for any kind of drama."

"Friends? How about soldiers?"

He held his drink up to her for a toast and she met his. "Soldiers, then." After downing the last bit of liquid, he set his glass on the mantle and offered his hand, bowing cordially.

She let him guide her back on to the dance floor and though he held her waist as they waltzed, she kept her distance and avoided looking into his eyes. When someone summoned the major after the music ended, and Frost asked her for the next dance, she relaxed.

"I leave tomorrow," Frost told her. "As does Major Billet."

"He leaves?" Her excitement escaped her lips much louder than she had anticipated. She held her hand over her mouth as Frost swiftly moved her across the room.

"Shh." He laughed. "Yes. They're sending him to France. Lucky dog escaped Burma, but in a sense, I'm glad we're going in opposite directions."

"Well, I will miss you. Can't say the same for him."

"My advice is that when you get out of the army, don't leave a forwarding address."

"Don't worry about that. I'll be Mrs. Morrissey by then, anyway."

Regardless of how beautiful the night had been, the stars, the music, the friendship, loneliness gnawed at Janet. When she returned home, she took out the letter she had started, and wrote.

Lou, My Darling,

Today has been the worst day yet. I'm afraid I have a severe case of missing you and of homesickness too. It seems impossible to believe that one year ago this time, the planes and ships were all on the move against France. The time has gone fast in looking back, but the last five months have really seemed an eternity, too. Wish I knew for sure just when we would be coming home. Really seems too much to hope for, doesn't it?

That you and I may soon be together again? That's all I'm waiting for anyway, darling. To feel your arms about me again. It's been so long.

 ... I have reached the bottom rung of despondency. There has been no mail from the States since the first of February. So, my morale has sunk out of sight. But my love for you grows stronger every day and I go to bed every night with the prayer that perhaps tomorrow!

 ... Lou, honey, how is your leg coming along?

 Chapter 37

April 1945

> *The free individual has been justified as his own master; the state as his servant.*
>
> —Dwight D. Eisenhower

Lou clung to the parchment in his hand and glanced out over the porch of his parent's home. The plum trees along the narrow road in front of the house had burst into full bloom. The sweet smell of their blossoms permeated the air. Though the skies were still gray, the temperature had risen, and forecasters predicted that spring had come. A chorus of birds flocked in the maple trees next to the house, and bees danced among the dandelions in the patches of grass along the sidewalk. Indeed, a time of new beginnings, new life being born, new love.

He read the delicate handwriting for the fourth time, finding comfort only in the fact that she wrote the letter, but not in the agony she expressed. He knew the same pain, had known the same heartache ever since he left England. The image of her beautiful face had become quite vivid in his mind. He meditated on the photographs she sent, so that her image wouldn't fade from his memory. He wanted her here with him, away from the war, in his arms. His desire to hold her and comfort her was unbearable. He told her these things in the letters that he wrote. That all these painful months apart would pass. All the agony they experienced now would soon be a memory. Someday they would sit together by a fireplace, sip hot cocoa and tell their adventures to their children.

She hadn't received his letters.

Lou my darling,

I went to a movie today. On either side of me were couples holding hands and talking and having fun, while the seat beside me was very empty. I felt so lonely that I didn't wait to see it all. Darling, I miss you so and love you so dreadfully much.

There are still a lot of rumors about leaving here for home this summer. Of course, there is nothing official, but I'm hoping.

Why haven't you written? Are you well?

Your loving Janet

What the doctors at Deshon had done for his leg had been miraculous. No amputation had been necessary, and he walked on it daily. With a cane, yes, but moving was much less painful than it had been in the past. His medical discharge papers were on their way, and soon he'd be a civilian. For a week, now, he lived in a civilian world at his parents' home, a welcome relief from the white sheets, white walls, and white masks worn by people who prodded him. No more medicine and hospital food.

How he longed for Janet's affection, her warmth, her touch, her gentle words!

His sister had come to visit, and his mother had sent him flowers and cards before he was discharged. His family, in their eagerness to make him happy found a girl they wanted him to marry. A friend of the family.

He argued with them and told them about Janet and that his heart belonged to the lovely nurse in England. But he was in a vulnerable position, and his mother was a strong woman. She refused to have anything to do with his "antics," as she called them.

"Nonsense. I'm sure whatever you and that nurse felt for each other was only a passing fancy. What soldier doesn't fall in love with his caretaker? Well, she's not taking care of you any longer. No, hon, we'll get you fixed up with Beverly. She's everything you could possibly want in a wife. She cooks, she cleans, and best of all, she's a civilian and not involved with any war. Time for you to be home. Get a job. Get married to a good wholesome girl. Raise a family."

Lou wasn't going to marry Beverly.

He had a dream that he shared with Janet and someday that dream would come true. Someday he'd be in Pennsylvania with her walking the deer trails. Neither those dreams, nor Janet would slip away.

"Louis Morrissey!"

His thoughts were interrupted when a familiar figure appeared walking down the sidewalk. Charlie Bowman all decked out in his neatly pressed uniform. A friend from his division who had been hospitalized with him. Charlie wore a broad grin as he skipped up the stairs and they shook hands.

"They let you out!" Lou exclaimed, glad to see him healthy again.

"I'm healed."

"And in uniform? What's up?"

"No sooner did the hospital release me than I got my marching orders. I'm headed back to Europe."

"Hey, I'm sorry. That's the pits!"

"It won't be so bad. The war's almost over, Lou. At least in Europe. Not much more to do there but clean up. I think that's why they're sending me. I'm handy with a broom!"

"Sit on the porch with me and have some coffee." Lou pulled up a chair for Charlie and slipped into the kitchen. "Where you are going first?" he asked, returning with a cup of steaming brew for his friend.

"Petworth."

Lou's heart skipped a beat. "No lie!"

Charlie took the cup Lou handed him.

"You're going to Sussex? How long will you be there?"

"Until they get me on a ship to France, I suppose."

This was an opportunity Lou couldn't let pass. "Do something for me, would you?" he asked.

 Chapter 38

Surrender

Dearest Lou,

I feel that life is at a standstill and everything is waiting, and I think of time as before I knew you and since you have gone. Everything in the future counts from when I see you again.

"Janet, they want you at mail call!"

"Why?" Janet's heart flew into a frenzy. She had all but quit expecting mail, and it had been too disappointing to see her friends and colleagues walk away with letters from home, and none for her. But when she raced to the group of soldiers circled around the delivery sergeant handing out packages and letters to the troops, she pushed through them.

"Castner?"

"That's me!"

"Ah! There you are!" the sergeant said. "Called you a couple of times. Come get this stack. It's weighing me down!" He laughed.

"A stack?"

"Looks as though some of these letters have been sitting in the office for a while. Major Everett sent them on for me to deliver to you along with today's mail. The one on top is dated February." He handed Janet a pile of letters bundled together with a rubber band.

She about fainted when she thumbed through them. Every envelope bore the return addressee as "Morrissey." Sue had to help her walk, Janet was so out of breath. Tears rolled down her cheeks. When they arrived back at their hut, Janet tore open the letter on top. With shaking hands and tears in her eyes, she read what she'd been longing to read.

Dear Janet,

I love you. I miss you and I am counting the days until you're here safe in my arms ...

"You mean these letters have been in the office all this time?" Marty asked. She thumbed through the stack on the table. "Look at this! Some of these envelopes are torn open. Major Billet was holding onto them all this time? Looks like he read them, too! That worm!"

Janet didn't care what Major Billet had done, anymore. He was gone, and now Lou's letters were in her hands and she'd sit down and read every one of them a dozen times. "I suppose it could have been an oversight."

"Right." Marty snickered. "Now that Billet is gone, this mail mysteriously shows up in one huge bundle. I knew I didn't like that man."

"Enjoy, Janet." Sue rubbed her back gently. "Never mind what might have happened. You've got your sweetie in your hands now and you've got some work ahead of you answering all those letters! You can have my ration of stationary."

Janet didn't answer. She barely heard her friends. She read that first line repeatedly, savoring it as a decadent dessert, imagining each word from his lips, his warm breath close to her ear.

Love letters.

Letters about his family.

How he met her sister, Flo, and had dinner with her parents. How his army buddies that were on furlough visited him in the hospital. How his leg was getting better and how much he hated being in hospitals. How they didn't have to amputate and now he could walk with a cane. How he was going to be moving in with his folks and then he'd find a job and get his own apartment. How his friend at the furniture store would offer him a deal when it came time to get a house. How he couldn't wait to see her when the war was over.

"If only I had gotten these sooner, I would have been so much happier!"

Someone knocked on the door and Sue answered it.

"Someone's here to see you, Janet," Sue said. "Janet?"

Janet wiped her face with a hankie and looked up at the man stepping into the hut. She'd never seen him before.

"Yes?" she said.

"Charlie Bowman, here, ma'am." He saluted.

Janet returned the salute as she rose from the bed, but said nothing.

"I'll get right to the point, miss. I know you don't know who I am, but Sergeant Morrissey asked me to stop by."

"Oh! Lou! You've seen him? In Ohio?"

"Yes, ma'am. A week ago. There was something he asked me to bring to you." The sergeant wrestled a package out of his pocket. Wrapped in paper decorated with tiny snowmen, torn at the corners, the bow smashed, having seen better days, he handed it to her. "I guess it was supposed to come at Christmas last year, but Lou didn't want to send it if you weren't getting his letters. Sorry that it's so tattered. It got a little messed up on the trip, but the box is still intact."

Janet unwrapped the package carefully, giving a quick glance at Sue and Marty, who looked curiously over her shoulder.

The paper fell to the floor, leaving a small velvet jeweled case in the palm of her hand. Tears of anticipation clouded her eyes so that when she popped open the lid, she could barely see the diamond engagement ring. She bit her lip, and fell back on the bed.

"Thank you for delivering this," Marty told the soldier. We'll look after her now."

Lou my darling,

It came today. It's beautiful. I'll cherish it forever and ever. Lou, I love you. I'm so excited. Thank you, dear. I'm indeed the envy of all the girls. I've got to get home soon to thank you personally. I love you, sweetheart. I can't even think of anything sensible to say. My heart is beating like a trip hammer! All I do is sit here and look at it sparkle and kiss it and wish you could have brought it to me personally. It fits, and I'm crazy about it. It's the most beautiful thing that I have ever had.

I love you forever,
Your wife-to-be, Janet

Epilogue

Written by Mary Morrissey Gardner

Janet boarded the *Queen Mary* and arrived at the harbor in New York in late August of 1945. She returned home to her family in Corsica, Pennsylvania where Lou was waiting for her. They were married on September 1st in Saint Nicholas Church in Cretes, Pennsylvania. The only member of Lou's family in attendance was his sister, Betty Morrissey, who had driven him there from Cincinnati, Ohio.

The honeymooners went to Niagara Falls for a very short time. Then Janet, new Army orders in hand, re-boarded the ship to be transported to a base in the South Pacific. However, before they set sail, the ship caught fire, and everyone had to disembark. It was at this time that Janet's letters from Lou were lost.

The new bride, on leave, took a train from New York to Cincinnati's Union Terminal Station, where she was met by her ecstatic bridegroom to wait for her ship to be repaired.

Before the ship was ready to depart, victory over Japan was declared, so the now civilian newlyweds, faced with the post-war housing shortage, settled into the family home on Saybrook Avenue, and stayed there for the rest of their lives along with their five children, Betty, and Grandma and Papa Morrissey.

Lou died in 1994 and Janet in 1999, both of lung disease. Janet had become a devotee of English romance novels and relived her English romance vicariously until the day she died.

So here it is, Mom, thanks to my wonderful, amazing sister-in-law, Dianne Gardner, your very own English romance story, based on your love letters to Dad (he kept everyone) and the stories you both shared with our family. It was written with love and admiration. –Mary

Acknowledgments

Thank you to the many people who helped bring this story about including Dick and Mary Gardner for all the letters, the news clippings, and the hours of reminiscing about your mom.
Thank you to Catherine Corry for help with the medical events, and for helping me research the WWII tools and equipment we needed to carry those scenes out. Thank you John Renehan for the wonderful map made exclusively for this story!
Thank you, Larry Fowler for the endorsement, and thank you my husband Steven (Michael) Gardner who encouraged me, and supported me during the process.

ABOUT THE AUTHOR

D.L. Gardner artist, author and screenwriter writes primarily fantasy novels including all sub genres. Her latest book is historical romance. She's a lover of the classics, both visual and literary and believes a story should be good enough to hand down from one generation to the next.
Winner of Book Excellence Award, Best Urban fantasy at Imaginarium Convention, and a host of screenings and trophies for the historical fiction screenplay Cassandra's Castle

Visit her website http://gardnersart.com for more information about her books, audio books, artwork and more
Other works by D.L. Gardner
Ian's Realm Saga
Diary of a Conjurer
Cassandra's Castle
Pouraka
Altered

D.L. Gardner

Thread of a Spider
Where the Yellow Violets Grow

CPSIA information can be obtained
at www.ICGtesting.com
Printed in the USA
JSHW081533190323
39138JS00003B/9